Chasing the Tail of Chance
(The tale of an Irish dog)

By Cindy Krieg-Nuttall
Illustrated by Janet Griffin-Scott

(A Production of Chance Encounters Enterprises)

Dedicated to the gentle giants I have loved.
Because of you, I know what it is to be
great of heart,
Humble of spirit and joyful for the dawning
of each new day.
I can not thank you enough.

C.J.

Believe!

I give thee a dog which I got in Ireland.
He is huge of limb
 And for a follower equal to an able man.

 Moreover, he hath a man's wit
  and will bark at thine enemies
  but never at thy friends.

 And he will see by each man's face
  Whether he be ill or well-disposed towards thee
  And he will lay down his life for thee.

From Icelandic Saga of Nial...

Noble Hounds.
A production of
Chance Encounters Enterprises,
2008.

Order this book online at www.trafford.com
or email orders@trafford.com

Most Trafford titles are also available at major online book retailers.

Note for Librarians: A cataloguing record for this book is available from Library
and Archives Canada at www.collectionscanada.ca/amicus/index-e.html

Photographic Collages for Dedication page, Running-dog page, Disclaimer, Noble Hounds, Shamrock
Graphics and The Champ Page by Angie Succee

Printed in Victoria, BC, Canada.

ISBN: 978-1-4251-8059-1 (Soft)
ISBN: 978-1-4251-8060-7 (e-book)

*Our mission is to efficiently provide the world's finest, most comprehensive
book publishing service, enabling every author to experience success.
To find out how to publish your book, your way, and have it available
worldwide, visit us online at www.trafford.com*

Trafford rev. 8/24/2009

 www.trafford.com

North America & international
toll-free: 1 888 232 4444 (USA & Canada)
phone: 250 383 6864 ♦ fax: 812 355 4082

Table of Contents

From over the rainbow . . .
From that place Beyond comes a dog,
His coat is black. And his heart is gold
And as he journeys across the bridge between
these two worlds,
He brings with him that glittering gem,
The promise of one more chance . . .

Chapter One ♣ *The Carousel*

On the edge of a great forest by a babbling broc
summer by red-and-yellow bleeding hearts, liv(
with brown hair and big, green eyes; green like s
the slate-grey rocks where she would sit and wai
go by.

Her name was Cindy...not Cynthia, and certainly no
... just plain Cindy, or C.J. which was short for Cind
lived in a pale yellow house with green trim and a fl
sometimes leaked when it rained - but not always.

She lived there with her Mom, who had brown hair a
green eyes like C.J., and her Dad, who was tall and
spoke in a quiet, gentle voice. She also lived there
baby sister Jo-Jo who had blue eyes and one golden cui
very top of her head.

There were no other houses around the pale yellow hous
green trim on the edge of the great forest, and no
children. So, C.J. would play alone by the babbling broc
at the back of the house where pink wild roses {
Sometimes, she would visit the groundhog who lived ber
the blueberry bush at the edge of the great forest.

Mostly C.J. sat on the slate-grey rock cut overlooking
highway, in front of the pale yellow house with green trim
the edge of the great forest. There she sat hour upon ho
watching the cars and trucks go by. Some went north an
some went south. Every one of them went somewhere. Ever
one of them was in a hurry.

Every once in a while, a face from inside one of the trucks or cars would turn to look at the little girl, with brown hair and green eyes sitting alone on the slate-grey rock cut. Every once in a while, someone would wave or honk their horn, and C.J. would wave back and wonder what it was like to be going somewhere in a hurry.

C.J. knew somewhere down that highway, there were towns and villages where houses stood huddled together in cozy rows, not alone like her pale yellow house with green trim at the edge of the great forest. She also knew that in those houses lived children who opened their front door each morning to find other children waiting to play.

It seemed everyone had someone, everyone but C.J.

Her Mom's days were busy with baby Jo-Jo, feeding and cleaning and cooing to the tiny body with the single golden curl on the top of her head. Her Dad had his job. He kept the highway in front of the pale yellow house and beyond safe so the cars and trucks could hurry by even in winter when blustery winds blew snowdrifts, in ghostly strands, across the ribbon of pavement.

Sitting on the slate-grey rock cut, C.J. tucked her knees up under her chin and hugged them close to her body. Right then and there, with the pure-hearted resolve known only to the very young or the very, very old, she decided she would wish the best wish ever - and she would wish it on the very next red car or truck that went by.

Why red? Well red was a good colour; next to green, it was her favourite.

So she waited and watched as the hours passed and the sun moved up in the sky to hang over her like a brilliant gold medallion dangling on the neck of a beautiful lady. As she watched the line of traffic going north, and the line of traffic going south, C.J. saw every colour in the rainbow, but nowhere was there any sign of something red.

Then, just as she heard the familiar creak of the old screen door of the pale yellow house with green trim at the edge of the great forest . . . Just as her mother's voice lifted like butterfly wings to float through the air finally settling on her ears, it happened!

Something red rounded the bend and headed right towards her.

Not only was it red; it was quite simply, the most marvellous 'something red' a little brown-haired girl could imagine even in her wildest dreams.

Up front was the biggest, the best, apple-red truck possible. It had long mirrors that stuck out to the side, chrome bumpers and running boards that glistened in the noonday sun. But there was more. C.J.'s eyes could not believe what came next.

On a flatbed trailer behind the apple-red truck was a painted carousel of prancing ponies. Each pony's knees was captured in high-stepping motion. Their brightly painted eyes laughed and their mouths opened just wide enough to show-off shiny metal bits and snow-white teeth.

C.J. wondered if anything, in the whole, wide world, could be lovelier.

"Mom, look! Look!" She shouted back toward the pale yellow house with green trim.

C.J.'s mother, holding baby Jo-Jo in one arm, cupped her free hand to shade her eyes against the sun, and smiled at the marvellous sight of the apple-red truck towing the prancing-pony carousel.

The driver of the truck, seeing the little girl with brown hair and green eyes standing on the slate-grey rock cut, pulled the string of his air horn and let out three sharp honks; so loud they made C.J. blink three times.

The driver smiled and waved at the little girl and the pretty lady with the baby standing in the doorway.

C.J. waved back. Even her mother waved and then called once more for C.J. before she turned and disappeared inside.

"Coming. I'm coming," C.J. called back to her mother.

The apple-red truck with the prancing-pony carousel had now passed C.J. by. As it slipped away down the ribbon of highway heading north to unknown destinations, C.J. closed her eyes, crossed her fingers, her legs and even some of her toes. (This was possible only because she was wearing sandals.)

Then flinging her arms into the air as if to touch the sparkling-medallion sun, she made the biggest wish of her very young life.

"Oh beautiful apple-red truck ... oh prancing ponies with your eyes so bright ... send me some special someone to be in my life."

As the shiny chrome bumper of the trailer, carrying the prancing-pony carousel, slipped out of sight, C.J. heard her mother calling her again; less patiently now.

C.J. turned towards the pale yellow house with green trim at the edge of the great forest. Her sandals scuffed up small puffs of dust leaving a solitary trail of footsteps in the gravel; as solitary as the life of a little brown-haired girl with no special someone of her own.

C.J. would never again see the apple-red truck or the prancing-pony carousel. She watched from her rock cut by the highway's edge, but the apple-red truck must have made its return trip late one night as C.J. lay tucked in her bed under the flat roof of the pale yellow house with green trim at the edge of the great forest.

But when she closed her eyes and tiptoed off into the land where dreams come true, it was there waiting for her. And so it would always be. The apple-red truck and the prancing-pony carousel would return, forever a symbol of the power of childhood dreams.

Chapter Two ♣ The Long Wait

The hopeful heart of a little girl, though cloaked in sweetness and giggles, is not a flimsy feather to be blown hither and dither with each passing wind. What shows on the outside may not even hint at the raging spirit within. So it was with C.J.

Each night when C.J. curled up beneath the blankets of her bed under the flat roof of the pale yellow house with the green trim at the edge of the great forest, she dreamed about the apple-red truck with the prancing-pony carousel.

In those dreams, the carousel stopped at the laneway of the pale yellow house with green trim at the edge of the great forest, but the magic ring of prancing ponies kept spinning 'round and 'round. The chimes dangling in the midst of their circling bodies tinkled like faery laughter teasing and taunting them on.

Then without warning, the ponies would slow. Slower and slower they would go until they stood absolutely silent and still. From the murky shadows, a vague form would appear. C.J. strained to see as her heart brimmed with the hope this might be her "someone special" stepping from the shadow of her dreams into her waiting arms.

But the phantom figure hovered in the half darkness never stepping into the light, and she'd wake to the sound of her Mom and baby Jo-Jo making morning noises in the kitchen.

Laying there in her little bed, C.J. wondered about the dream and if today would be the day her marvellous wish would come true.

As the days flew by on the calendar, she held bravely to hope. As the greens of summer gave way to autumn's russet cloak, she believed. Even as November's barren trees reached up to the grey, flat sky, she did not doubt.

But as the first faltering flakes of snow drifted to earth, C.J. still sat alone on the slate-grey rock cut. With her hat pulled down over her ears and her scarf up over her nose, she watched cars and trucks hurry north. Still others hurried south. And for the very first time, C.J. wondered if her wonderful wish would ever come true.

It was in this state of heart she sat down with pencil in hand to write to the wisest person she knew - her Nana Jean, who lived far away in Ireland, a mythical land of leprechauns, shamrocks and pots of gold at each rainbow's end.

She shared with Nana Jean the story of her encounter with the apple-red truck and the prancing-pony carousel. She told her of her wish ... her wonderful wish for someone special of her own.

With her heart on her sleeve, she asked that wise woman from across the ocean the one question she most wanted to hear the answer to ... "Nana if I really, really believe, can my wish ... my most wonderful wish, come true?"

C.J. asked her Mom to help put Nana's address on an envelope. Then she put the letter inside and stuck three stamps on the front. That was just the right amount to carry her letter all the way across the deep, dark ocean to Ireland. Finally, C.J.'s Dad took the envelope, and dropped it in the mailbox on his way to work one day.

Then C.J. did what she was getting to be very good at indeed. She waited.

Chapter Three ♣ *Believe!*

One day C.J. came in from playing under the giant pine trees that sheltered the pale yellow house with green trim to find a letter waiting on the kitchen table. Her heart leapt as she recognized the lovely flowing penmanship on the envelope from past birthday and Christmas cards.

Best of all, the letter was address not to Mom ... and not to Dad. It was to Miss C.J. She scooped it up with both hands and hugged it to her heart. As she did, the sweet scent of spring lilacs drifted up to greet her.

C.J. put the envelope to her nose, and inhaled deeply. Just for a moment, she could see her Nana's smiling face lined with years of life and love; a soft grey curl gone astray and hanging by eyes that twinkled like the stars in the night sky.

C.J. took the letter to her bedroom and sitting in her little purple rocking chair by the window that overlooked the stream and the forest beyond, she carefully opened the envelope so as not to let it rip.

The letter was full of the talk that nanas and little girls share when they open their hearts one to the other. Then at the very end came the words C.J. had been waiting for.

"As for your most wonderful wish ... Oh my darling child, there is only one way for such dreams to come true. You must first learn to believe with your heart in the things the human eye can not see. It is really that simple. Believe my darling ... Believe!"

C.J. let the letter drop from her hands. It fluttered down to rest in her lap. There she sat in her little purple rocking chair staring out the bedroom window of the pale yellow house with green trim at the edge of the great forest which by now was nestled under a deep blanket of snow.

As C.J. watched plump snowflakes drift dream-like to earth, she again clutched the lilac-scented letter in her hands and whispered to the distant sky beyond the million falling snowflakes ...

"I believe Nana. I do believe."

That night C.J. slept with Nana's letter under her pillow and visions of prancing-pony carousels in her head.

While C.J., her Mom and Dad, and baby Jo-Jo slept, the winds dancing around the pale yellow house with green trim at the edge of the great forest began to howl like lost souls who could not find their way home.

Gentle snowflakes, caught up in the wind's wild rhythm, performed a whirling dervish, and the snow piled deeper, and still deeper, on roads, on trees and on the pale yellow house with the green trim at the edge of the great forest.

Chapter Four ♣ *In From The Cold*

The barren branches of trees blown together by the winter wind made a lonely sound like fingernails scraping across a chalkboard, only worse.

Even tucked safe and sound under layers of blankets, the sound made C.J. shudder. For a moment, she thought about creeping down the hall to her parents' room.

She thought how nice it would feel to slip under the covers beside them. How safe it would feel to lie between her Mom and Dad listening to their steady breathing in the night. But she was a big girl now. So instead, C.J. pulled the blankets higher 'til only her eyes peered out from over them. Glancing around her room, C.J. watched as familiar bedroom furniture turned into a roaming herd of eerie creatures in the yellow haze cast by the nightlight beside the dresser.

Laying there, she thought of the prancing-pony carousel again and wished with all her heart that her "someone special" would find her soon. Then she wouldn't have to lay here alone listening to the winter wind make the trees sing such a sad song.

When you're laying still in the darkness, all the tiny noises in the world grow large. The ticking of the clock, you didn't notice before, sounds like a hammer. The refrigerator motor whirs. The furnace 'thunks' to life and warm air gushes forth from floor vents with a 'whoosh'.

C.J. lay there tuned into those many tiny sounds. Together

they made-up the undercurrents of life inside the pale yellow house with green trim at the edge of the great forest. Outside, Mother Nature unleashed her fury.

Suddenly, C.J. sat bolt upright.

What was that ... a scratch at the front door? Then came something else. Another sound ... what was it? Something soft and asking ... something like ... a whimper?!

For a moment, she could hear nothing but the pounding of her own heart in her ears. C.J. hugged her pillow like it was her best friend. Then sitting very still, she listened once again. She held her breath so she could listen harder.

The wind howled. The tree branches rubbed together. The furnace blew air up the vent in her room, 'whoosh'. The fridge whirred on and on. And C.J. sat there in the dark listening as hard as she knew how.

Just when she thought the wind had been playing tricks ... just when the rapid beating of her young heart had slowed to a steady thu-thump-thu-thump, it came again!

"Scratch ... scratch" and a whimper so weak, it was like a fading wish.

C.J. leapt from her bed and as her feet hit the floor, the hall light flicked on and light flooded through a crack in her half-open doorway. She could hear her parents speaking in tones of hushed urgency. They'd heard it too!

"Mom?" C.J. called in a quiet voice so as not to wake baby Jo-Jo. "Mom?" She called a little louder; still no answer.

C.J. opened her bedroom door a bit; just enough for a little girl with brown hair and green eyes to slip quietly through and move like a shadow down the hallway toward the light.

The overhead kitchen light was on. Bright shards tore through the velvet cloak of night in the hallway where C.J. held back soaking up every sound like a sponge. It was very late and she knew she should be tucked in bed and not wandering the house, but curiosity made her bold like a cat.

She held back in the shadows listening to muted conversation and movement she did not recognize. Finally, she could wait no more. Skewing up her courage, C.J. rounded the corner and came face first into her parents' backs as they huddled over something on the floor. She stopped seconds short of a pile-up.

It was a strange sight. Her parents crouched on the floor; their bodies bent together protectively. Mom made comforting sounds like when she rocked baby Jo-Jo to sleep. Dad was shaking his head back and forth slowly and tutting; the way he did when something was wrong.

Her parents were so absorbed by whatever lay on the tile floor of the kitchen in the pale yellow house with green trim at the edge of the great forest that they didn't hear C.J. tiptoe up behind them.

They didn't hear her climb onto the kitchen stool by the wall; all the better to see what it was that had come in from the cold on this blustery winter's night.

Then suddenly, like a curtain parting, her parents shifted and in the opening between their bowed heads, she saw the most marvellous something, the most "special someone" her eyes ever beheld.   This was even better than the prancing-pony carousel.

C.J.'s breath caught in her throat. Her eyes lit up like shooting stars ripping a path across the night sky. There wrapped in her Dad's green parka was a jet-black puppy. His sleek coat was wet and glistening. His eyes were shut. He did not move.

C.J. crawled off the stool. She didn't see her parents watching. She only had eyes for the black pup on the floor in front of her. She was beguiled. C.J. knew one thing and one thing only. She had to touch! And so she did.

Her plump child's hand with the little dimpled knuckles reached down to stroke the glistening black coat. As she did, the puppy lifted its weak and weary head to meet her hand with the lick of a rose-pink tongue. As brown eyes met green, C.J. felt something odd, like a hand on her heart giving a little squeeze.

 The feeling was strange, but not bad. In fact, it made her want to laugh out loud, and cry at the same time. Sometimes it can happen that you meet someone for the first time, but it feels like you've known them an eternity; which is a very long time. That's how this was.

As if they somehow understood, C.J.'s parents stepped back

and with their arms around each other, they watched their little brown-haired girl sink to the floor beside the puppy. Like metal drawn to magnet, the puppy snuggled in closer to the little, brown-haired girl until they lay pressed together like pieces of a puzzle, pieces that needed to find each other to finish the picture.

Outside Mother Nature raged on. But inside the pale yellow house with green trim on the edge of the great forest, two hearts sparked a flame that would burn long and true.

C.J. imagined above the raging wind she could hear, ever so faintly, the tinkling chimes of the prancing-pony carousel. She knew in her pure child's heart that her most wonderful wish had at long last come true, and that Nana Jean had been right all along.

"When you believe in things only the heart can see, your dreams can come true," C.J. smiled and buried her nose in the sweet scent of damp puppy.

Chapter Five ♣ *Two Hearts*

"C.J.... C.J."

Her mother bent over gently shaking C.J.'s shoulder.

"The puppy needs to sleep now and so do you. You can see him in the morning," she said softly pulling C.J. to her feet. "Poor little man. He's exhausted from being cold and afraid."

"Mom, can we keep him?" C.J. said holding her Mom's hand as they headed down the hallway to her bed. Looking over her shoulder, back to the kitchen, C.J. could see her father covering the puppy, and stroking his head before dimming the lights. The puppy slumbered fitfully, whimpering now and then at the snow monsters stomping through his dreams

"C.J., he must have his own family somewhere. They're probably heartsick that he's missing. So don't get your hopes up kiddo. OK?"

A lump rose in C.J.'s throat. Her arms and legs felt rock heavy as she dragged herself back to bed. She couldn't even speak. She just looked up at her Mom with moist eyes and her Mom looked back and smiled an understanding smile.

C.J. knew in her heart that the sweet puppy wrapped in her Dad's parka was no mistake. He was sent to the door of the pale yellow house with green trim on the edge of the great forest to be her special friend. He was her reward for believing for so long that this day would come.

After a gentle brush of lips against C.J.'s troubled forehead, her

Mom hurried off with a muted rustling of nightclothes to quiet baby Jo-Jo's restless infant noises now rising from the darkness at the end of the hall.

Little by little C.J. heard the people noises go still. Then slowly the house noises crept back out to play. Once again, there was the familiar ticking of the grandfather clock in the living room like a heartbeat, steady and true. It played bass to the 'hum' of the florescent light over the kitchen sink and to the 'whir' and 'whoosh' from here and there throughout the pale yellow house with green trim at the edge of the great forest.

The only people sound now was the rhythmic breathing of her parents in their room down and across the hallway. Finally, they were asleep. C.J. was not.

Barely daring to breathe, she slipped from between the warmth of her sheets. Her bed was warm and safe but there was a powerful force pulling her down the hallway. The cold hardwood floor chilled her toes. C.J. shivered all over. Her heart beat hard as she crept back down the hallway.

Finally she stood in the kitchen doorway staring in wonder at the sight of her "someone special" curled up in a furry black coat and swaddled like a baby in her Dad's very best green parka. C.J. dropped to her knees.

As if she still could not believe her eyes, C.J. reached out a hand half afraid it would fall on thin air ... half afraid her heart's desire was only a restless dream on a stormy winter's night.

Then she felt the glorious sensation of damp hair between her plump child's fingers, and she knew it was true. The puppy's weary eyes did not open as she stroked him softly, but the 'thunk-a-thunk-a-thunk' of his tail against the floor said, "That's nice ... So nice!"

"Thank-you for finding me. I've been waiting such a very long time. What took you so long, anyway!?" C.J. whispered into one slightly damp ear.

There in the stillness of the night with her very "special friend", C.J.'s world shrank down to the sweet scent and rhythmic breathing of the slightly damp pup she held so gently against her. The beating of the puppy's heart made the whole world feel safe and sure.

It was like when she was very little and Mom rocked her to sleep. She hoped lying there, feeling her heart beat back at him, that the puppy understood he was safe now too.

"You will never be out in the cold again," she whispered.

A pink tongue flicked out to wet her nose and make her giggle. Then and there, an iron pact was forged as two hearts fell in league to beat as one.

Though the sky may rumble and the earth may quake, in all of existence, there is no greater force than this.

Chapter Six ♣ *Morning Magic*

Magic still exists in the world.

It is found in the patter of Santa's reindeer on snowy rooftops. It is found in the tooth fairy's lilting touch as she trades coins for the lost teeth of children left under pillows with hope and wonder.

Magic lives in the blue bells that bloom in early spring under the old walnut tree and in the smile of a little girl with brown hair and green eyes resting her head on the shining, black coat of her very own "special someone".

Even before C.J.'s baby sister let out her first wails of woe at the break of dawn ... before Dad stumbled in the half-light of the hallway to the bathroom to shave ... C.J. slipped on her snowsuit, mitts, scarf and boots. She took her beautiful black puppy out into the freshly-fallen snow so they might make their mark on the new day ... on this fresh beginning ... together.

The night's dervish had settled into lazy drifting flakes. Crystal diamonds on the blanket of fallen snow glistened in the light of a golden sunrise.

Though wobbly-legged, the puppy bowed at the girl inviting her to play. She bowed back and then fell over in the snow flapping arms and legs to make a snow angel. The puppy rooted his nose in billowing snowdrifts and came back up wearing a frosty white mask.

Standing there in the wake of this new day – this new beginning - C.J. looked at her pup, the twinkle in his eyes and the tilting of his perfectly sculpted head. He was so proud, sweet and pure. C.J. had never seen anything so lovely. She doubted she ever would.

As C.J. stood there unable to look away, she realized the puppy's deep brown eyes were also drinking in her eyes of green. Some people live a lifetime and never know what it is like to collide with a kindred spirit this way.

The door of the pale yellow house with the green trim at the edge of the great forest opened a crack and C.J.'s mother called out anxiously, "C.J. ... C.J."

"Mom, look! Look! He's sooo beautiful!"

Her mother stopped in the doorway, her housecoat pulled tight against the morning's chill, to take in the moment; this very important moment in her daughter's life. It was a moment so significant that C.J. would use it for the rest of her life as a measuring stick to size up all else.

Watching child and puppy together in a pristine world under the cleansing light of the new day, C.J.'s mother felt great joy. The world can greedily demand a parent's full attention leaving nothing to spare. While tilting at the world's windmills defining moments in a child's life - moments that will not come again - can vanish into the void.

But not today.

"Oh yes C.J., I see. He really is beautiful," C.J.'s Mom said this from the deep well of her heart. "But come inside now. Bring your friend. It's time for all puppies and little girls to eat breakfast."

C.J. smiled and thought how much she loved her mother and

the way she always understood.

"Come on boy. Let's go." C.J. called to the pup.

Black beauty against white world, the puppy bounded forward then suddenly pulled up with a yelp. One paw came up and dangled like a broken thing with no will of its own. C.J.'s heart contracted hard and fast like an arrow had pierced it through.

"Easy boy, easy ..." she called out. Her legs could not move fast enough through the deep snow to carry her to his side. Finally, she was there. With care, she put one arm under his chest and other across his back.

"Let me help," she whispered in his ear. And he did, remarkably putting his faith in a love so very new. He rubbed his velvet muzzle against her face; which in the Language of Dog means, "Friend!"

Together they trudged through the deep, deep snow toward the pale yellow house with green trim at the edge of the great, snow-covered forest. Not the cold nor the snow nor the pain in the black puppy's legs could stop them.

In this vast, crazy world, girl and pup had found each other. How wonderful could life possibly be?!

Chapter Seven ♣ *Along Comes A Friend*

All the way to the vet's clinic, C.J. cradled her new best friend's head in her arms.

Usually when Mom stayed home, C.J. sat up front with Dad. She would smile and wave to the people who lived in the little village down the highway from the pale yellow house with green trim at the edge of the great forest, and they would wave back. C.J. loved country life. Everyone smiled. Everyone waved. Everyone knew you.

Today, C.J. chose to sit in the back seat with the great black pup instead of up front. C.J. held the pup close so he could feel her heart beat. She wanted him to know it beat for him. The pup knew. He lay still relaxed and trusting in the harbour of her arms.

Before they set out, C.J.'s Mom had again gently explained the puppy must belong to someone. She did this looking deep into the innocence of her daughter's green eyes, and holding softly the little hand she so loved.

"When his people are found, the pup has to go. You understand don't you?" she had said.

C.J. thought her Mom looked as if she would cry. She touched her Mom's face with her soft child's hand, and said, "Don't be sad."

She felt sorry her Mom could not yet understand that this pup came to her compliments of the prancing-pony carousel and a little girl's wish that was strong and true. He was anything but a mistake.

'Believe ... believe in things you can not see,' Nana Jean had said.

Well, C.J. had believed. She had believed through summer, fall and winter too. And finally, on a blustery night there had been a scratch at her door. Now, in spite of her parents' doubts, C.J. believed with all her heart that this black pup had come to stay.

C.J.'s Dad signalled then swung the car off the highway past a roadside mailbox painted bright yellow and stencilled with brown paw prints across the side. The name on the mailbox read 'P. Peters, D.V.M.' which C.J.'s Dad explained stood for doctor of veterinary medicine.

Passing along the narrow laneway was enchanting. Cedar branches bowed under the weight of the fresh snow. Crystal prisms strewn across the snowy surface twinkled like faery dust and chickadees and sparrows darted from bough to bough.

"Wait here," C.J.'s Dad said sliding from behind the steering wheel. She leaned forward a bit watching him climb the front porch steps of the log house where Dr. P. Peters D.V.M. lived and worked.

Next thing C.J. knew, her Dad was back at the car. He leaned inside and scooped the pup effortlessly into his arms. C.J. knew how good that felt. She remembered the day she crashed her bike. He was there, out of nowhere, to scoop her into those same safe arms.

Now he reached a gloved-hand back to take C.J.'s red-mittened hand. She took it and smiled up at him. Together the three – man, child and dog - made their way to the door of the log house. Before their feet hit the first step, the door flung open wide. Dr. P. Peters stood there smiling, all six-foot-and-more of him.

"Ohhh my! What have we here?" he said; his deep voice drifting out into the cold, white world. Gentle hands took the pup from C.J.'s Dad. The pup snuggled into the vet's ginger-coloured beard and made little grunting comfort noises.

"I do love a cuddler." Dr. P. Peters smiled and nuzzled the pup right back.

"Come inside. Come in out of the cold," Dr. P. Peters said to C.J. and her Dad. "Let's see what we can do for this handsome little man."

Dr. P. Peters towered over C.J. and her Dad. His twinkling eyes made you think he might share a funny story any minute. Sometimes, he did!

Placing the pup on a metal table in one of two examining rooms in the clinic, Dr. P. Peters turned his attention to his patient. "OK little man, I need you to tell me where it hurts."

"He can't talk!" C.J. said.

"Oh but he can!" said Dr. P. Peters. "Just watch."

C.J. and her Dad stood silent on the sidelines watching Dr. P.

Peters listen to the puppy explain, in the Language of Dog, what exactly was wrong. Fortunately, after years of relentless study, Dr. P. Peter's was an expert in canine conversation in all of its many and diverse dialects.

Turning to C.J. and her Dad, Dr. Peters explained that People Talk, while quite impressive on some levels, depends entirely on words and words can be twisted and have more than one meaning.

By comparison, he went on to say, the Language of Dog is sublime ... a degree of change in the expression of the eyes, a tensed muscle, a lowered head, a jaw tipped up, an ear cocked forward or back... all these have meaning to someone familiar with Dog Talk.

Finally, Dr. P. Peters turned to face C.J. and her Dad. The pup lay happily on the table watching his new friends.

"What you have here is a very special pup and I'll tell you why," Dr. P. Peters said.

C.J. tugged at her father's sleeve. "See Dad ... Special!" Dr. P. Peters smiled and tousled the top of C.J.'s head.

"I am a hundred per cent certain, this is a purebred Irish wolfhound puppy ... umm, maybe about four to five months old," he said shining a light inside the pup's mouth to see his teeth which can tell a vet about how old an animal is.

"As I said, Irish Wolfhounds are very special."

C.J. smiled and her Dad just said "Really?" mostly because he didn't know what else to say.

"Yes, they are," Dr. Peter's continued. "Where did you say you found him?"

C.J.'s father told the story of the pup's unexpected appearance at their door the night before. C.J. stood quiet as a mouse. She knew this was probably not the time to talk of prancing pony carousels and her wish for a special someone of her own.

"So you think he's a purebred Irish wolfhound? Even stranger then him being out on his own on such a terrible winter's night," said C.J.'s Dad. "And what's up with his legs?"

C.J. could contain herself no longer. "Hey Dad, he's Irish. Get it? Irish, like Nana Jean! "

Inside, she thought, this was all the proof she needed. It was her Nana, her Irish nana, who told her "to believe". She had believed and the pup had come.

"Well then, this is a strange co-incidence. Here let me show you something," Dr. P. Peters said pulling a book from the top shelf of an antique oak bookcase in the corner of the room.

Thumbing through the pages, he stopped and slapped the book down on the side counter. He gestured for C.J. and her father to come closer. Standing on her tiptoes, C.J. could just see the picture of a giant hound with a square head, round muzzle and the kindest eye, and there was even a poem about an ancient Irish wolfhound called Nial.

"This is a full-grown Irish wolfhound. This dog is a giant; the tallest of all the dogs in the world," said Dr. P. Peters. He paused to read their reaction before going on.

"How tall are you C.J.?" he asked. She looked up at her Dad with questioning eyes.

"Hum, I think last time we measured, she was about 45-inches tall," said C.J.'s Dad.

"Well the full-grown, male Irish wolfhound can stand from 34 to 38 inches at the withers. The withers is this bony area at the bottom of the neck," he said, pointing to the picture in the book. "That's just a little bit shorter than the top of your head. So a full-grown wolfhound would be taller than you are right now."

"Whoa!! That's tall!" C.J. said. She looked at her little black pup and tried to imagine him standing over her looking down.

"It's tall alright," said Dr. P. Peters. "And what it means is that this sweet, little puppy has a lot of growing to do. Sometimes that's when things can go really wrong for these giant dogs. It could even be that's what's happening with this fella right now. To be sure, I need to x-ray his legs."

C.J.'s Dad rubbed his chin and looked at the floor.

"Sounds expensive. You know we want to help but this isn't even our dog. We're going to put up flyers around the village, and here at the clinic if it's OK. We can do what we can in the meantime to keep him comfortable, but anything else ... well

...I don't know." He shook his head.

Her father's words shredded C.J.'s dreams. She closed her eyes, and inside her head said Nana Jean's words over and over again. "Believe ... Believe ... You must believe!"

"I don't want to alarm you, but you may be on a wild goose chase looking for this pup's former owners," said Dr. Peters.

C.J.'s Dad looked puzzled. "How's that?"

"Come here, I want to show you something you may not have noticed," he said.

"OK little man, let's stand up," Dr. P. Peters supported the puppy as he stood. "I want you to look at the joint just above this puppy's paws on the front legs."

C.J. looked. Her Dad looked. They saw big knobby joints but nothing strange.

"OK to the untrained eye, it is hard to see what I see. But look closely," said Dr. Peters. "The pup's toes point out; not straight forward, and the angle of the bone from the joint to the foot is more sloped than you might expect."

"Now this could be just an awkward stage of growth. Often pups will show these signs and in a few weeks things start to straighten up again. They can even get pain that goes along with the growth spurt. So maybe this is just a stage. Maybe . . . There's always that chance. "

"On the other hand ... there is a serious condition in which the two long bones in the front legs grow unevenly. I would be wrong not to tell you this could also be what your pup ... or rather ... this 'found' pup has."

He paused for a moment, stroking his ginger beard, searching for the right words.

"There is no easy way to say this, but someone may have abandoned this pup knowing he had a problem."

"You can't be serious," C.J.'s Dad said.

"You wouldn't believe the things you see in a veterinary practice. To some people, animals are disposable. Really what they should be is a life-long commitment."

Hot red spots burned on C.J.'s cheeks. She hated the world of man that would take a creature as beautiful and pure as her pup and throw him away like trash.

She went to her pup laying there on the examining table so confident ... so innocent, and she hoped he didn't understand the cruel Language of Man. He nuzzled her ear with a wet nose. If Dr. P. Peters was right, she tried to imagine the hard face of the person who could turn this pup out on a cruel winter's night to die alone in the cold.

She knew this: there should be a law to make such a person pay. For a moment, no one spoke. C.J.'s Dad stared out the window at the snow that had started to fall to the ground in lazy fat flakes.

"If ... and I mean 'if' we decide to take in this puppy, what exactly are we getting into here?"

Like her Dad, Dr. P. Peters spoke slowly, carefully choosing his words. When he finally came out with what he had to say, his words made C.J.'s young heart sing.

"If it's what I think, it will take a big commitment ... but I'll tell you what. If you decide to keep this boy, I will do everything I can to help. I have a real soft spot for Irish wolfhounds. Yes, I have," Dr. P. Peters said ruffling the black pup's head. He took his wallet out flipping to the photo section.

"Look here," he said crouching down to C.J.'s level. "This is Miss T." C.J. stared at the blonde shaggy face of a wheaten-coloured wolfhound.

"She was our first wolfhound. My wife and I loved her very much, but Miss T got a terrible illness and died last year."

C.J. saw the softening of Dr. P. Peter's gaze. For a moment, he drifted to another place. She knew right then and there that he had loved the beautiful blonde Irish wolfhound in the photo as deeply as she loved this pup.

She tugged at his sleeve; three gentle tugs. He crouched down until they were nose to nose. Only then she whispered ever so softly into his ear.

"It's OK to cry when you're sad." He tweaked the nose of the little brown-haired girl and laughed.

"Yes, it is," he said smiling. "You know I think you just might be the right one to help this pup and I will do what I can to help you help him. OK?"

"Super OK," C.J. said.

 "Well then listen up … First, we try some diet changes and rest for the leg. No running for two weeks."

"Got it! No running for two weeks. "Did you hear that boy?" C.J. said to the black pup, who sat patiently watching, his eyes as big as the pancakes Mom made some Sunday mornings.

C.J. and Dr. P. Peters turned at the same moment to look at her father. Now, it was up to him. For a breathless moment the world hovered between light and dark.

"I think I'm outnumbered here," Cindy's Dad said. "OK. OK. We will try this but we still have to put posters up just in case somebody out there is looking for him. That is the right thing to do. Agreed?"

"Agreed," C.J. said. She even took her Dad's hand and shook on it. That was good enough for this brown-haired girl and a black pup who had come by chance to her door at the edge of the great forest on a cruel stormy night.

Chapter Eight ♣ *Peas in a Pod*

As if there were magic beans in his kibble, the puppy grew and grew and grew! C.J. grew too, but not as fast.

In the doorway between the kitchen and living room, C.J.'s Mom carefully measured her sprouting height every few weeks. With her back against the wall, C.J. would stand still as her mom balanced a ruler across the top of her head. Then, using a green pencil crayon, her Mom would mark, measure, and date the wall.

Some weeks C.J. grew. Some weeks she did not. The great, black pup always grew.

C.J. would hold the pup's green collar so he would be still when it was his turn to be measured. This puppy was growing every bit as fast as Dr. P. Peters said.

C.J. had her Dad take a photo of her smiling and hugging the neck of her beautiful big black pup. She put the photo in an envelope and sent it on a long journey to her Nana Jean's home far off in Ireland.

When the old woman opened the envelope from her little granddaughter in Canada, she looked at the photo of the smiling child and the big, gentle dog.

She smiled too and said, "Aye! Now there's a match!"

She put the photo in a frame by her easy chair in the living room of her tiny house which was part of a row of tiny houses on a street made up of row upon row of tiny, brown houses.

Many long lonely hours, she would sit and stare at the photo of the child and the great dog. It filled her heart with joy. Even from thousands of miles away, she could see this child and this pup belonged together. From an end table drawer, she pulled out a faded photo of a red-haired girl hugging a black Irish wolfhound.

"Ah Nell, what a bonny lass you were. We were peas in a pod, just like these two. We were indeed."

Closing her eyes, the wee Irish woman held close to her heart the faded photo and relived those glory days when she and Nell were young of limb and high of spirit wandering the dales and glens about the small Irish village where she was born.

Sometimes things are truly meant to be. All the posters, C.J. and her Dad had placed on telephone poles around the village advertising the found Irish wolfhound pup had by now blown away in the restless winds of the changing season. Those that still hung on bulletin boards around the village were faded.

For awhile C.J. would stop, and listen, and hold her breath every time the phone rang. But no one called and no one came. Meanwhile, the great black pup and the child grew taller and closer with each passing day. In fact, they were inseparable.

Dog and child played inside the pale yellow house with the green trim at the edge of the great forest and they romped together in the yard and the surrounding forest.

When C.J. sat at the dining room table, the pup sat under her chair, his chin on her lap. When dinner was served, C.J.'s Mom put the pup's food on a stool beside C.J.'s chair.

"Eat up children," she would say with a wink and a smile. Baby Jo-Jo, sitting in her high chair across the table banged her tray with a tiny, tight fist, and said "Eat! Eat!"

One night C.J. ate dinner at a friend's house. The pup could not be consoled. He ignored the food in his dish and took up a position across from the kitchen door. At exactly 7:07 p.m., C.J. burst through the front door of the pale yellow house with green trim at the edge of the great forest.

The pup was so delighted at the sight of her that he wriggled all over and his tail went 'thunk-a-thunk-a thunk' on the hardwood floor with a joy he could not contain.

C.J. giggled and hugged his neck. As she dropped to her knees beside him, the pup licked her hand. At last, he dove into his dinner and bits of kibble flew here and there. When he was done, C.J. filled up his water dish and, kneeling before him like a subject before royalty, she held it while he drank.

C.J.'s Mom and Dad agreed they had never seen anything like it. Watching the dog and child at play made them smile.

And when C.J. put her weary heard on her pillow and snuggled under her downy duvet, the pup curled up on his own soft bed on the floor beside her. Sometimes when C.J.'s Mom softly said "good-night darling" and closed her bedroom door, C.J. would pat the empty spot on the bed beside her twice.

Up the pup leapt and together they would drift off to the land where all things are possible and dreams most certainly can come true.

Chapter Nine ♣ *His Name is ...*

Finally one day when the warmth of the sun offered the first promise of spring and melted the remaining patches of snow, C.J.'s Mom and Dad called her into the living room. Padding along into the room on her heels, came the great black pup.

The pup and C.J. sat and looked at the two grown-ups. Baby Jo-Jo slept in her room down the hall.

"Well C.J., I guess it's time," said C.J.'s Dad.

"Time?" C.J. said with a question in her voice. Her hand stroked the pup's head as she spoke.

"Time to name that pup of yours. If he's going to stay, he needs a name," said C.J.'s Mom.

"Yes!" C.J. cried clapping her hands together.

"So, kiddo, any ideas?" her Dad asked.

C.J. just smiled and buried her face in the sweet smelling coat of her very best friend. With that black coat of his, he could have been a Blackie, or Ebony or even a Midnight, but he wasn't.

This black pup, who came to the pale yellow house with green trim on the edge of the great forest to be her special someone, had to be called Chance.

It was chance and a wish from the pure heart of a child cast into the whirling centre of the prancing pony carousel that brought him to her one stormy winter's night. So Chance would be his name.

"Chance," she said it out loud for the first time.

"Chance. I like it!" said C.J.'s Mom.

"Works for me,' said C.J's Dad. The great black, pup, now known as Chance, wagged his tail as if to agree.

Chapter Ten ♣ *The Crossroads*

Sometimes just when life is good and the sun is shining brightly in the bluest of blue skies, storm clouds are gathering just out of sight.

Once again Chance lay on the metal examining table in Dr. P. Peters' office. Dr. P. Peters stood with his back to C.J. and her Dad. He was staring at x-rays on a lighted, display table. They were x-rays of Chance's legs.

Suddenly, as though he'd finally found the right words, Dr. P. Peters turned to face them.

"OK first the bad news. The front legs are bowing and we should think about treatment ... possibly surgery," he said.

C.J. felt her mouth go dry. Her hands felt sweaty. She walked over to Chance and protectively put a hand on his paw, as if her touch was all it would take to keep him from harm.

She was afraid to even look at her Dad. She did not want to read what was in his eyes.

"As I explained earlier, young Irish wolfhounds grow so fast at different times during their first year of life that things can go wrong. Growing an Irish wolfhound puppy takes great care and a dash of luck."

Dr. P. Peters stroked his ginger beard thoughtfully and then continued.

"I am sorry Chance has this problem. I am sorry for him and I am sorry for all of you who love him, but don't lose heart. Never lose heart."

There were unsaid words hanging in the little examining room in the back of Dr. P. Peters' clinic. They felt like the weighty air of a sultry summer day just before a million rain drops burst relieving the clouds of their great burden.

C.J. and Chance were ushered from the room by Marian, Dr. P. Peters' wife and partner at the clinic. Her special touch was everywhere, but mostly it was there in her eyes and the earnest tone of her voice.

She always took time to speak a kind word, and there was something in her smile that whispered "There, there ... It will be alright."

Sitting in the waiting room C.J. hypnotically stared at the tropical fish in the aquarium as they drifted in and out of their water-plant jungle. C.J. and Chance strained to make meaning out of the murmur of voices behind the closed door.

Their urgent whispered tones made her afraid. Sitting on the cold tile floor, C.J. hugged Chance. The world felt colder than the winter storm that had blown Chance into her life.

Chapter Eleven ♣ *Run-A-Ways*

Back home that evening, C.J. and Chance had their bath, their biscuits and a bedtime story. After their busy day, they should have drifted off easily to dreamland, but this night, sweet dreams would not come.

Tonight, these two hearts, entwined, could not find their way to that sheltering place. C.J. lay in the quiet darkness of her room straining to make sense of the whispered and worried voices down the hall. More whispered voices!

Finally, she slipped from between the covers and tiptoed down the hall. She knew they were talking about Chance. She needed to know what was being said. Chance shadowed along at her heels.

Bright light shone from the kitchen where C.J.'s Mom and Dad sat with cups of coffee in front of them. C.J.'s Mom had been crying. There was a box of Kleenex on the table and crumpled tissues everywhere.

"Maybe it would be better this way," her Dad said, reaching across the table to take her hand.

"Maybe if she just woke up, or came home one day and he was gone, it would be better than her watching him fall apart. You know we can't afford expensive surgery. "

"But she loves him ... she loves him ... '' C.J.'s Mom choked back more tears.

To herself, standing there in the shadowy darkness at the edge

of the hallway with Chance's cold nose against her hand, C.J.
said loud enough so only she and Chance could hear.

"I do. I really do love him." But she didn't cry.

There are defining moments in everyone's life. Sometimes
those moments find us even as children. They leave us standing
at a crossroads with two ways to go. The choice we make will
determine who we really are.

C.J. knew she could crawl back into bed. Under the warmth of
her duvet, the world always seemed safe. That would be so
easy, but then what would happen to her friend, her Chance,
with the dawning of the next day?

As much as she loved them, C.J. was wise enough to know her
parents didn't understand about she and Chance. She doubted
there were any words she could find to change that.

Even at this tender age, C.J. knew there's a time to sit back and
a time to get busy. This was a "get busy" time, and she knew
now what had to be done.

In the early morning light, as C.J.'s Mom lifted baby Jo-Jo
from her crib and headed down the hall to start the coffeepot,
the world had already changed. She just didn't know it yet.

As she got the toaster, the bread and the butter out, the world
seemed as right as rain. The steady hum of life, in the pale
yellow house with green trim at the edge of the great forest,
was familiar ... and comfortable.

But when C.J.'s Mom opened her little girl's door at 7 a.m. to call the child and Chance for breakfast, an Arctic chill swept out the open door.

It filled every room in the pale yellow house at the edge of the great forest with the whispered fear that things would never be the same. The little room where Chance and C.J. slept was empty. Child and dog, two pure hearts thrown together by chance and bound by love, had evaporated into dawn's shadowy half-light.

Far across the ocean in Ireland, Nana Jean startled and spilled her morning tea when the photo of her dear granddaughter and the great black pup teetered at the table's edge for a moment and then crashed to the floor. The glass smashed into a thousand pieces.

"Oh my!" she exclaimed. "Oh my!" she repeated pushing herself up from the comfort of her easy chair. No time to sit back now. She had a mission. "Hang on my darlings, I am coming." She went to her closet and began to pack for the long voyage ahead.

Chapter Twelve ♣ 'The Truth about Water and Wolfhounds'

Long after C.J.'s Mom and Dad stopped whispering and finally shuffled down the hall to bed, C.J. lay thinking.

She had taken the duvet off her bed and lay on the floor, her head resting against Chance's shoulder. The steady rise and fall of his breath soothed her fears.

C.J. loved her Mom. She loved her Dad. She loved baby Jo-Jo, but if Chance couldn't be here anymore, then neither could she. By the time the first fingers of light chased the dark from the sky, C.J. and Chance had left behind the pale yellow house with the green trim at the edge of the great forest ... perhaps forever.

In the soft mist of dawn, child and dog set out to face a world that was much larger and stranger than either could possibly imagine.

They took with them a jar of peanut butter, a box of crackers, some dog biscuits and a pocket full of high hopes; the latter being the single most important ingredient they would need for the journey ahead.

They kept to the trails and the shadowy edges of the forest like the deer and the other wild creatures of the woodland world. Every so often, C.J. would see Chance limp on his twisted front legs. Even though he never once whimpered, C.J. saw and when she did she pretended it was she who needed rest.

During those moments of respite, they made a strange and

lovely sight, little brown-haired girl in the pea green sundress and the big black dog – biggest in the world when full grown -

with his noble head resting in her lap.

Once they watched quietly as a graceful blue-grey heron strode soundlessly through the creek bed on legs as thin as twigs.

Like them, she was following the winding creek that emptied into the very place they were headed, the great blue lake beyond.

Sometimes, just like that creek, the road we head down in life is longer and more winding than we can possibly imagine. It was that way for a little green-eyed girl and her black Irish wolfhound pup.

They had to make it to the lake. C.J. thought: "It's our only hope."

C.J. had a plan. She would find her cousin's wooden rowboat in the brush at the side of the lake where she'd seen him store it. Part B of the plan was to row from there across to an island where her Aunt had a cottage.

An island seemed like a safe place to hide. They could stay there until the storm clouds passed and the world was safe again for Chance, or until the food in the pantry ran out, which ever came first. Either way, C.J. didn't want to even think how long that might be.

The trip to the dock along the shores of Shaggy Lake seemed short when travelling in the back seat of her Dad's car listening to tunes on the radio and watching scenery slip by. It was a different kind of trip on foot.

By lunchtime, C.J. and Chance reached the park-entrance road. When the attendant was busy signing in an overnight camper, the run-a-ways ducked past the small toll hut.

They slipped like shadows into the sheltering arms of the majestic, white pines along the camp road; those great sentinels of nature who see all and yet speak not a word.

"Shhh," C.J. whispered to Chance. "Tiptoe like this."

There is nothing quite as ridiculous as the sight of an Irish wolfhound doing his level best to be invisible. C.J. couldn't help herself. She laughed ... but not out loud.

"Good boy Chance!" He wagged his tail, as always, pleased that she was pleased.

Fallen pine needles underfoot were soft and sweet. In the shade of a particularly wise, old white pine, the pair stopped to rest their weary feet and enjoy a modest snack.

"Not much farther now Chance." C.J. sat down beside where Chance lay. She patted the black pup's head. His eyes closed. It was way past his morning naptime.

C.J. was tempted to curl up beside him and sleep on the soft, forest floor strewn deep with sweet-smelling pine needles. She wanted the prancing-pony carousel to carry them away to a safe place, to a world that understood the importance of the friendship between a child and a giant black pup.

She wanted to be somewhere people understood what she and Chance had was worth fighting for. But that wasn't happening and there was no time to rest.

She had to get them to the dock, across the water and onto the island before nightfall. There they would find shelter, food and water. She had seen her aunt leave the key to the cottage under a rock. If she could get them there, she could get them in.

As they padded along a wooded forest trail headed to the boat launch, C.J. worried what they would do if the rowboat wasn't there. But it was! Just as she remembered! It lay upside down in some brush to the side of the trail. The oars were tucked up under the wooden seats.

"Great!" she said with delight. "Look Chance! Look!"

Always happy to please, he wagged his tail and sniffed around the boat. Then he looked up at C.J. as if to say, "Well that was interesting. Now what? Umm?! Now what?!"

Dragging the rowboat to the shore took all the muscles C.J. had and a few she was only just discovering. She wiped her brow with a sense of accomplishment. As C.J. popped the oars into their fittings, she whistled for Chance to stop his sniffling around and to come. He did, but then things got interesting.

Wolfhounds by nature are not water dogs. That is not to say some don't enjoy the occasional splash in the lake in the heat of a summer's day, but only when it's their idea. So, when C.J. asked Chance to hop into the rowboat, abandoning the safe platform of Mother Earth, he grew roots.

"You gotta trust me boy." C.J. said. Chance stepped forward tentatively. Then, with a whimper, he backed off.

"OK, take your time Chance. Hey, I understand. I've been afraid before too. I used to be afraid to go down a slide. Then I tried it and, you know what!? It was great! Maybe you'll like a boat ride, if you try it. So what do you think?"

Chance cocked his head this way and that way, listening to the sound of his best friend's voice; reassuring words, but anxious tones. His Dog Talk brain was assessing it all. In the meantime, his great paws remained rooted to the spot where he stood.

"If I go first, will you try?" C.J. clambered into the rowboat. The front was resting on the shore. The rear bobbed up and down in the water.

Chance inhaled in fright and backed a step further away. He bwoofed a "bwoof" of warning. His fear was both for himself and for his friend ... his very best friend.

Suddenly C.J. felt the weight of the world come down on her child's shoulders. She bowed her head into her hands and sobbed.

There was no one to help. No Mom. No Dad. Darkness was not far off and she was only one little girl trying to save the pup she loved.

C.J. looked up as she felt the boat rock gently to and fro. Standing in front of her, in the boat, was Chance. His eyes were clouded with doubt and he looked puffed up from holding his breath in fear.

"Alright! Good boy!" C.J. said, and Chance gave her a big sloppy kiss that started at her chin and ended at her forehead. She wrapped her arms around the big shaggy neck and dried her tears in his beautiful black coat.

"Thank-you, Chance. Thank-you."

C.J. sniffed back a final tear, took a deep breath and started to row. Chance sat watching with less fear now and more curiosity. In a few moments, he lay down in the bottom of the boat with his head on C.J.'s foot.

C.J. rowed and rowed and hoped the sun that was hanging low in the sky would take its time slipping into the dark glassy surface of the lake.

C.J. rowed and then she rowed some more. Chance watched wishing he could help, but, of course, there are some things even Irish wolfhounds can't do.

C.J.'s Dad had always pointed out all the lake's navigational landmarks as they traveled these watery channels to her Aunt's cottage. Now, as C.J. rowed, she replayed those earlier trips and his words in her head.

'Look for the white buoy with the two red stripes. Steer clear of the shore going through the channel to avoid running up on the sharp rocks lurking below.'

'Head to the far shore and when the yellow cottage with the green shutters comes into sight, veer right. The shoreline bends and as it does the island comes into view and there perched on a rock cut standing tall over a sandy beach is the cottage that looks like a giant A.'

This unusual cottage that looked more like it belonged in the alphabet than on this rocky shore would be a safe harbour for a feisty little girl with brown hair and green eyes and her great black wolfhound pup named Chance. First, they had to find it.

Rowing across a lake is different than zooming along in a motor boat. Soon C.J.'s arms felt like rubber. The sun was dipping its bottom half into the deep, dark waters at the horizon where sky and water meet. Her heart was sinking as fast as the sun.

"What have I done, Chance? I don't know if I can find the way in the dark." Her shoulders slumped and the oars bobbed in the water as the boat drifted freely in the lake's currents. "I'm just going to rest Chance. I just need to put my head down on my knees and rest ... just for a moment. Then I'll row so hard that we'll get there before you know it."

Chance listened, tilting his head this way and then that as if it would somehow help him understand her words. As the sun slipped away, the air chilled. C.J. shivered and clutched her arms around her.

The pea-green sundress offered little warmth against the evening's chill and the terrible weariness she felt. Finally unable to warm herself, C.J. dropped into the bottom of the boat to huddle close to Chance who was always warm.

The ripple of waves across the water gently rocked the rowboat like a cradle. Before long, C.J. and Chance dropped off to sleep. In her dreams, C.J. saw her Nana Jean's face and heard her voice say one word. "Believe!"

Sometimes the world can be cruel; other times, fate castes a smile without warning. The little rowboat could have drifted into open water in the dark and been struck by a powerboat speeding by. It could have run onto rocks sending dog and child into frigid waters to their certain death.

Instead, like a mother with a weary child, 'Fate' rocked the pair into a peaceful slumber on friendly currents that carried child and great black pup past the white buoy with the red strips. It carried them safely through the rocky channel, across to the far shore, beyond the yellow cottage with the green shutters.

Finally, it carried them onto the sandy shore at the foot of a rock cut; the very rock cut on which sat the cottage that looked like an 'A'.

Chapter Thirteen ♣ *'A' Cottage*

Still sitting in the little rowboat, C.J. rubbed the sleep from her eyes and stared up the embankment at the cottage shaped like a giant 'A'.

Now that they were here, she wondered if she had made a mistake. The cottage was not as she remembered, full of happy voices and laughter. There was no golden light flooding out to break the heavy veil of night.

Tonight the cottage looked like a hollow husk. Like the shell after the peanut has gone. Its inky windowpanes were like empty eyes staring coldly into the night. And for the first time C.J. knew, it is not the place that makes the people but rather the people who make the place. C.J. swallowed hard to break the grip of doubt.

She thought about the pale yellow house with green trim at the edge of the great forest. She wished for the normal sounds of Dad coming through the front screen door weary from work and ready for dinner. The sounds of Mom moving around the kitchen, pots clanging, food sizzling on the stove top, baby Jo-Jo cooing away to her tiny brown bear "Boo".

How C.J. wished she were there, safe and loved in the world she knew. Just then a great paw came to rest on C.J.'s knee. Chance was watching her, his head cocked to the side in a way that said, "What's up? ... Umm ... What's up?"

C.J. looked into those deep brown eyes and remembered why she was here on this shore with night falling around her darker than any night she could recall. She had to be brave for Chance.

"Hey little man, it's OK. It's just different than I remember ... " Glancing up at the unwelcome face of the cottage that tonight looked like an angry giant letter "A", she added under her breath so Chance couldn't hear " ... really different!"

The great Irish wolfhound pup and the little brown-haired girl in the pea-green sundress clambered out of the rowboat. The 'out' was clearly easier for Chance than the 'in' had been.

They carefully picked their way up an earthen path cut across the face of the rock cut. Up they went. Up and up the steep, rocky incline. Some cedar trees had made this barren patch their home. Their roots lay across the path like long boney fingers.

'Like witches' fingers,' C.J. thought and then shivered a shiver that went through to her toes.

Once or twice, Chance stumbled along the way. C.J. would hear him slip and turn to see him struggling back to his feet without so much as a whimper or complaint. And she thought, 'his legs are getting worse'.

To him, she said, "Way to go Chance. You're the best ... the absolute best. We're almost there. Come on boy, hang on!"

Finally they stood on level land at the top of the rock cut. There were exactly seven flagstones in the walkway leading to the side porch of the cottage.

She counted each flagstone. Then she went to the third stone from the porch steps, and crouched down. With her chubby child fingers gripping the edges of the cold, flat stone, and the wet earth from under it sinking under her fingernails, C.J. bit her lower lip in concentration as she tried to lift stone number three.

It was the smallest of the seven stones but still quite heavy for a little brown-haired girl who had that very day taken on the world with only a giant black pup with bad legs, by her side.

She grunted and groaned. C.J. felt more wet earth slide underneath her fingernails, but the stone did not move.

She flopped down on the earth and buried her head into her tucked up knees. When she looked up the giant black pup was standing in front of her so his big, wet nose was almost on her forehead.

"What's up now?!" his deep brown eyes asked.

"The stone is too heavy Chance," C.J. said. "I can't lift it."

Chance, who had been playing nearby with a large stick, trotted back to fetch his prize and bring it to her, thinking such a marvellous prize was sure to bring his best friend cheer. Back he came with his crooked little trot, and the stick teetering comically this way and that way in his mouth.

"Hey boy, you might just have something there." C.J. said. As she watched him parade his prize stick, she had an idea.

C.J. called Chance to her and said, "Give". Chance backed away a step, his eyes filled with mirth. "At last! Play!!"

He bowed down with his front paws and stuck his wagging tail high in the air. The language was clear ... "Let's play!"

C.J. put her hands on the stick. Again she said, "Give" but this time louder and in an even-more-serious voice. Chance, who could take a joke, thought it was all part of the game. Finally, C.J. gave a little tug just to show she meant business.

They say 'it's all in the timing', and I guess they're right because at the exact moment Chance decided to 'give', C.J. decided to 'take'.

C.J. hit the ground with a kind of a hollow 'umph' sound as the air shot out from her lungs. For a moment, she lay flat out on the ground clutching the stick to her chest.

Next thing she knew, there was a giant paw planted on either side of her head and she was being buffeted with wet wolfhound kisses. No one could ever possibly have been more adored or more soaked.

"Okay ... enough ... enough," C.J. said giggling. Rising to a sitting position, she wondered how she could fear anything in this world with a friend such as this by her side.

Using the stick, C.J. found she could raise the flagstone just enough. As she reached underneath, she felt what she was looking for. It was a little metal box that rattled when you shook it. The rattle was the key. The key was the way in. It would unlock the cottage door and give child and pup a place to lay their weary heads awhile.

C.J. dared not even think what tomorrow might bring. She only knew, it would be a tomorrow with Chance by her side, and that was worth fighting for.

There was no electricity in the cottage that looked like a giant letter 'A'. Her aunt and uncle used oil lanterns to create the golden light that shone from the cottage on those evenings when friends and family gathered there. The problem was C.J. had been told never to play with fire.

Deciding she had probably broken enough rules for one day, she instead rummaged through drawers looking for a flashlight. Just then, Mother Nature wrapped these two tired travellers in a radiant embrace.

The clouds parted and the full moon beamed across Shaggy Lake blazing a pearly path across the water, onto the shore and through the big picture windows of the cottage that looked like a giant letter 'A'.

Giant black Irish wolfhound pup and little brown-haired girl curled up together on a couch bathed in soft moonlight. There they sat and ate the meagre remains of the snack C.J. had packed that morning - a lifetime ago - back at the pale yellow house with the green trim at the edge of the great forest.

They drifted off into a deep sleep, curled together in the moonlight as though they had not a care in the world, for they had what each cherished most - each other.

Chapter Fourteen ♣ *Irish Hope*

Sleep did not visit the occupants of the pale yellow house with the green trim at the edge of the great forest that long night. Even baby Jo-Jo fussed in her crib long after her usual sleep time.

C.J.'s Mom and Dad were worn with worry but too frightened for their little brown-haired girl and her great black dog, to even think about sleep.

Hearts that know great love, can also know the aching void of great loss. C.J.'s Mom sat in her little girl's room holding Gray Rabbit, a floppy-eared stuffed rabbit C.J. held each night as she slept. A tear spilled from the corner of each eye as she ran a hand across a wrinkle in the cover on C.J.'s bed. She wondered where her darling child slept that night, and if she slept safely.

A sharp knock at the door made her jump. She dropped Gray Rabbit to the floor. His soft cotton-stuffed body hit the hardwood floor without making a sound.

She rushed for the door with every step hoping the late caller was a wee girl in a wrinkled pea-green sundress with a great black puppy at her side bearing apologies and a tale of the day's great adventures.

By the time she got there, C.J.'s Dad had already opened the front door.

There under a beam of light from the porch lamp stood not a wee child, but a wee woman with greying red hair worn in tight curls. She carried a large tapestry travel bag in one hand and leaned slightly on the handle of a wooden walking stick carved into the head of an Irish wolfhound, a black Irish wolfhound.

"Mother!" C.J.'s Dad exclaimed.

"Jean!" C.J.'s Mom exclaimed.

"Aye!" the wee woman answered in the thick rich accent of the Emerald Isle. "And where is my babe ... and where is her great pup?" C.J.'s Nana Jean asked tilting her chin up to better see her son.

She raised her walking stick with the Irish wolfhound head and tapped him twice on the chest. "She's not here, is she?"

"How do you know that? How could you possibly know? I don't understand," C.J.'s Dad said.

"Ahh son! Did I teach you nothing? There are powers afoot greater than yourself. Or did you think yourself the wisest of God's creatures to tread this mortal sod?"

Even through her tears, C.J.'s Mom had to pucker her lips to keep a smile from getting out. She loved Nana Jean. And she didn't care how it was she came to darken their doorstep on this gloomiest of nights. She only knew that this tiny Irish woman brought something they desperately needed right now. That precious commodity was hope.

C.J.'s Mom put the kettle on the stove to brew tea and the three adults, joined by their love for a little brown-haired girl, sat around the kitchen table. Together they formed a circle of love that might be strong enough to mend the rip in their world.

Sipping her tea, Nana Jean listened to the tale of the little brown-haired girl and her Irish wolfhound, Chance. She closed her eyes and imagined her granddaughter's love for the great black wolfhound.

"You do know son that the wee one must have overheard you talking about sending the pup away ... or worse?" she said.

With eyes so clear that they could have been the sky on a crisp winter's morn, she gazed hard at her son.

"Do you not know she's over the moon about that pup?"

"Mother that pup will break her heart. He's sick and we can't afford the surgery he needs. Even if we could, there's no guarantee it can save him. I will not let her heart be broken watching him fall apart."

"Son, it is you ... you ... not that pup who has broken this child's heart. Can you not see these two, this child and this great black pup, are beings whose spirits entwine? It was no mistake this pup came to your door that cold and stormy winter's night. It was destiny ... his destiny and C.J.'s destiny."

"These two are joined by greater powers and no earthly force has the right to tear them apart ... and that, my dear includes you!"

"Anyway, did you think you could protect her from the world's rough edges? We are here to live and experience it all ... the good and bad. How can this child grow strong and wise if you, with your misguided love, won't let her live in the real world?"

The room fell silent, except for the hum of the fridge and the ticking of a clock somewhere down the hall. All eyes stared down at teacups as if the brown aromatic brew within held some clue.

"Aw well. So be it. Now let's set about putting back together that which has come unglued," said the wee woman from the Emerald Isles.

And so they did.

Chapter Fifteen ♣ Last on the List – The Lake

The list was not long.

In C.J.'s short life, her travels had taken her to the village, to the park where the swing and roundabout were. They had visited Auntie Vi's pretty white house with the lovely lilac hedge that in the spring was a bounty of purple blossoms.

The flowers were so beautiful that you wanted to pause and enjoy them no matter how busy your day because as everyone knows lilacs, like Irish wolfhounds, only live a little while and so must be enjoyed while they are here.

The only other place C.J. had been in her short life was the island. But how would a child and a giant black pup with bad legs get from the mainland to the island on their own? So it was the last place anyone thought to look.

Finally, when C.J. was not here and was not there and in fact, could not be found anywhere, the island was the only place left to look.

Nana Jean, who had a special way of knowing things that others did not, clapped her hands on the kitchen table when C.J.'s Mom finally said, "You don't think they could have found their way to the island, do you?"

"No. No way could those two make it across Shaggy Lake to the island," said C.J.'s Dad.

But a pallor spread across C.J.'s mother's face. She sank into her chair. "What if they tried? What if they tried and didn't make shore?"

C.J.'s Dad held her hands in his and looked her straight in the eye.

"Don't even think that. Not for a minute," he said trying to sound so brave ... trying to sound sure.

Nana Jean reached out and laid her wrinkled hands upon the two sets of clasped hands.

"Hush, my darlings. Be still. I know what you fear, but these old bones of mine feel things and I am telling you, they don't feel the lake has taken our babe and her heart hound."

Their eyes met and the two frightened parents found courage and comfort in the wee Irish woman who had come from so far to be their strength.

Pulling a lilac-scented hanky from her sweater pocket, Nana Jean wiped a single tear from her daughter-in-law's cheek. Then supporting her chin with one gnarly finger and staring deep into teary eyes, Nana Jean said simply, "Believe child. You must believe."

Chapter Sixteen ♣ *Misty Morn*

C.J. awoke to the call of the loon cutting through the misty air that hung over Shaggy Lake. Today, the lake lay flat and still ... gray and heavy. The diamonds that only yesterday danced merrily across its surface had gone back into the Sun's secret chest of jewels.

Chance still slept. He lay at the opposite end of the couch curled up nose to tail as dogs sometimes do. Right now in the early morning light, he looked really quite small for a giant.

C.J. slipped quietly off her end of the couch and out the side door to find the outhouse. The little wooden hut stood just off the main path opposite the cottage. The red shutters on the side window made it look cheery. And the crescent moon carved on the door gave this little out-side toilet a personality all its own, and its occupants a view.

Chance raised his great black head and gave a stretch as C.J. came back through the screen door. This time his expression asked, "Breakfast?!" When you live long enough with a dog, you come to know every look has a meaning and every meaning a look.

C.J. took out the scant remains of the food she had packed into her little purple knapsack and laid it on the couch between them.

So they dined, little brown-haired girl and her giant black pup, sharing the slim pickings of the day. But when Chance had eaten the last bite, he reached across to lick C.J.'s hand as if to say "More ...?!" 'More' was something they didn't have.

C.J. thought about mornings in the pale yellow house with green trim at the edge of the great forest. She thought of waking in her bed to the comforting sounds of Mom making breakfast down the hall and Dad playing with baby Jo-Jo who had finished her bottle and now demanded to be entertained.

She had stepped such a long way outside that safe circle of love. But then again, it was love that had brought her here; love of a giant, black pup named Chance. That love had brought them this far, but now what? That was a problem she needed to think on.

So they sat, child and pup huddle together, on the couch in her Aunt's cottage that looked like a giant letter 'A', which by the way, was a lot less scary in the light of day.

They sat together as C.J. pondered the big question of the day, "What now?" ... "What now?" ... "What now?"

Chance simply sat lost in this lovely moment with his person – his very best friend - by his side. Dogs, unlike humans, know the moment you are in is really what matters most.

As they sat and looked at Shaggy Lake still covered in morning mist, the bow of a white boat slipped soundlessly through the dream-like haze. It was shrouded in mist, and so it took a moment for C.J. to process that it was real.

The motor was off and the white boat glided softly toward the dock. As it pulled alongside, it thunked a hollow thunk against the dock's black-tire bumpers. The sound repeated in rhythmic waves.

"Bwoof ... Bwoof," said Chance.

C.J. didn't know whether to be afraid or happy. She decided it was perhaps OK to be a bit of both.

"Shhh Chance," she said, laying her plump child's hand on his muzzle.

"But why?!" his eyes asked.

Holding in a bark is as hard for dogs as holding in a sneeze is for people, but for C.J., Chance would try. Chance cocked his head this way and then that way, watching the strange things his best friend did next.

C.J. dropped off the couch and crept to peer over the edge of the windowsill of the great window of the cottage that looked like a giant letter 'A'.

The figure approaching the path up to the cottage was quite small and moved with halting steps. "Tap-tap-tap", the sound beat out a rhythm that matched each footfall. "How strange! What is that?" C.J. wondered.

She turned back to see what Chance was doing. He'd heard it too. He craned his neck as if it would help him hear all the better. Every muscle was taut. His lips trembled as he tried to keep the "bwoof" lurking just behind his teeth from escaping.

When C.J. turned back to the window, she couldn't see the figure anymore and the sound had stopped. But then her heart jumped when she heard a footstep and a tap on the first step of the porch.

She crab-crawled backwards to where Chance lay, and pressed her body into his, never taking her eyes off the screen door. Still the noise came – one step ... two steps ... three steps ... four ... Then came the creak of the old screen door slowly opening.

C.J. sucked in her breath and buried her head in Chance's soft black coat. His great head rested protectively on her much smaller head and in that instant C.J. thought 'What other friend would be so brave?'

Then at the very moment, C.J. thought dragons would descend, it rained down shamrocks and sunshine instead.

"Ah my darlings, there you are ... together, as it should be, and safe, thank the heavens!" Nana Jean said crossing the room with slow deliberate steps accented by the tap-tap-tap of the wolfhound-head walking stick.

"My darlings, you have led us on a merry chase," and she laughed as only the Irish can, clear and true as a church bell.

C.J. couldn't believe her eyes or ears. Nana Jean here! How could it be?! Then a fine finger, gnarled from the work of years of caring for others, brushed a lock of hair from C.J.'s eyes and she knew it was true.

"Nana Jean," she gasped in wonder. "Nana Jean!" She fell into the old woman's arms.

"Ah yes. Even the brave of heart get weary and must fly home to let their tired wings mend," she patted the child's head and held her to her heart. But then this child was always there, right beside her heart even when oceans stood between them.

"And child, tell me, who is this?" Nana Jean asked stroking the great brow of the giant black pup.

"Oh Nana Jean, this is Chance!" C.J. said his name as if she were describing the most amazing treasure in the world, which in fact, she was.

"Hello you treasure you. So you are the one my grand-daughter is over the moon about. Well, I guess I can see why."

Caressing Chance's lovely coat, Nana Jean said, "It appears you are a hound worth fighting for. The war is not yet won but if I have anything to say about it will be. It most definitely will be!"

C.J. pulled back suddenly serious.

"Mom and Dad are going to send Chance away." Her voice cracked with emotion.

"I know child. I know. We have our work cut out for us, but nothing worth having in life is ever won easily. Someone as special as Chance, well, it takes a really special effort to make that dream come true. Trust me and ..."

"Believe," C.J. said at the same time as her Nana Jean. They shared a knowing smile.

"Now we have to go pay the piper, for your parents have been worried sick and you shall have a thing or two to explain, I am sure."

Chapter Seventeen ♣ Miles From OK

So in the end, C.J. didn't need to think about what came next. The new day brought its own answers. Perhaps this is the reason dogs are clever enough not to worry today about tomorrow. They know there are forces at play greater than any plans they may make.

C.J. gathered bits of this and that into her purple knapsack and taking her Nana's hand, started toward the door. Chance did not follow.

"Come on boy. Home." She put down the knapsack and patted her knees then opening her arms wide as if she were about to hug the whole world, she called, "Chance come."

Chance tried to rise ever so slowly. Then he stopped. Flinching, he closed his eyes to hide the pain as he collapsed back onto the couch with a whimper. Concentrating all his energy into this one effort, he tried once more. Again, he fell.

A deep gripping sob ripped from the back of C.J.'s throat. "Oh no! No!" She ran to Chance and flung her arms around his neck. He dropped his head onto her shoulder and closed his eyes as if this girl with so much heart was all the medicine he needed.

They stayed that way for a moment – child and dog lost in each other. Then C.J. felt her Nana's hand on her shoulder.

"Child you must run quickly. Get your father. He is down at the dock waiting for us. I will stay here with the big lad. The big lad knows he can trust me."

Slowly C.J. released her hold on Chance. He looked her in the eye and kissed her nose. It was his way of saying, "It's OK."

C.J. ran as fast as her legs could carry her. She ran through the screen door. 'Creak' and 'bang' it went behind her. She ran down the steps and over the rock under which she had found the key for the cottage that looked like a giant "A". She slipped once in the mud going down the slope to the dock.

"Dad! Dad! Come quick! Chance is hurt!" C.J.'s Dad crouched down, so he could look her in the eye. "What is it? What's wrong?" he asked.

His big gentle hands held her at the waist. Tall, quiet man and little brown-haired girl ran hand-in-hand down the dock and across the beach. At the pathway, C.J.'s Dad scooped her up onto his shoulders and she sailed above the world like a creature of the air.

Once along the way, C.J. bowed her head close to her Dad's ear and whispered, "I love you Dad. I'm sorry. I'm really, really sorry."

"I know little Pip. Believe me I know."

It was a peculiar procession that misty morning: an old woman leaning on an Irish-wolfhound-head walking stick, a brown-haired child all tousled and covered in mud and a tall, quiet man carrying a great, black pup down the steep path leading away from the cottage that looked like a giant 'A'.

It seemed to take forever to get to the waiting boat. C.J.'s Dad had tied the rowboat to the power boat so it could be returned. The power boat rocked as they each stepped on board.

Nana Jean closed her eyes and pulled her sweater around her. The weight of the past two days was now settling upon her. C.J. crouched on the floor of the boat beside Chance.

"It's OK boy. It's OK." She cooed to him over and over patting his side. But they all knew they were miles and miles away from OK.

The knowledge was a heavy weight that kept them silent the rest of the way home to the pale yellow house with the green trim on the edge of the great forest.

Chapter Eighteen ♣ Rings.....
and Other Precious Things

The pain of someone we love always cuts deeper than any pain we feel ourselves. As Chance tried bravely to endure the pain in his front legs, C.J. wept.

"You see. Look at this!" C.J.'s father said to his mother. "This is what we hoped to spare her."

"My darling boy," the wee Irish woman said, looking up at her son from over glasses perched on the end of her nose, "I hope you did not give this child life only to deny her the right to live it. There is pain in life, but there is also hope. Our little lass will be fine."

C.J.'s father flung his hands in the air and left the room. He could never win an argument with this iron-willed woman.

And so it was, the very next day, C.J. sat in the back seat of the family car with Chance beside her. Nana Jean and her Dad sat up front.

Dr. P. Peters was expecting them. He must have been watching and waiting because the front door of the log-house clinic flew open before C.J.'s Dad had even shut off the car engine.

With a few short strides of his very long legs, he was in the parking area and opening the rear side door. Stooping his six-foot-and-more-tall frame down, he peered inside.

Chance's tail went "thunk-a-thunk-a-thunk". Chance always recognized a friend when he saw one.

"Ok little man; let's see what all this fuss is about."

In one sweeping motion, the great kind man took Chance up in his arms as if he were a mere kitten. Everyone else piled out of the car and paraded inside with Dr. P. Peters and Chance in the lead.

Nana Jean stopped, leaned in close to C.J. and whispered ... "Oh, him I like!"

Chance didn't even look back when Dr. P. Peters took him in to the x-ray room while everyone else sat on pins and needles in the waiting area.

The clock on the wall ticked. Nana Jean tapped her Irish-wolfhound-head walking stick. Time dawdles like a turtle travelling uphill when the fate of someone you love hangs in the balance, and all you can do is wait ... and wait ... and wait.

When Dr. P. Peters emerged from the mysterious back rooms of the clinic, Chance was not with him and he had lost his smile somewhere inside.

He pulled up a chair and sat facing C.J. and her family. For a moment, he looked down at his feet as if to buy time. They all knew he was searching for the perfect words; but sometimes there are no perfect words. Sometimes there is only the truth.

Finally he looked up and simply said, "It's time." He gave his words a moment to sink in. Then he continued.

"Chance has suffered serious deterioration of his joints. He needs surgery and he needs it now."

C.J.'s father looked away with a far-off gaze wishing himself anyplace but here where he held in his hands a decision he knew could break his daughter's heart.

"Come here. I want to show you," Dr. P. Peters said.

He led them all into an examining room. Chance lay on a blanket in the corner. A veterinary assistant knelt beside him idly patting his head. Chance wagged his tail in greeting but did not try to rise.

On the opposite side of the room, strange photos hung in front of a flat light. These were Chance's x-rays ... pictures of his bones.

"Here's the problem right here," Dr. P. Peters said, pointing to x-rays showing the long bones in Chance's front legs.

"For Chance to walk, these long bones must be the same length. You can see they are not, and that puts stress on his joints. Enough stress will make the joints break down. "

Sucking in a big breath of air as if trying to clear his head, Dr. P. Peters continued.

"Chance is a big dog. He has no future if he can't walk."

Dr. P. Peters turned to look C.J.'s Dad right in the eye. "Do you understand what I'm trying to say here?"

C.J.'s father's face was ashen and frozen in sadness. Finally he spoke, and when he did, his voice was flat and empty.

"I understand alright, but there's nothing I can do. We can't afford expensive surgery ... I wish I could."

Then turning to C.J., he said it again ... "I wish I could Pip."

"Pip I think you should go wait outside," he said. This time he couldn't even look at her.

There was such a heavy, silence in the room. No one looked at each other. No one spoke. It was even hard to move your arms and legs.

C.J. positioned herself protectively between Chance and the three adults. She knew they were thinking the unthinkable. If they couldn't afford to fix him, there was only one other thing these grownups were thinking. She couldn't let that happen.

"Good heavens!" Nana Jean exclaimed. The lyrical lilt of her Irish tongue and the strength of the great heart beating within this wee woman's frame broke through their suffocating fear.

"Look at your faces! One would think it was the end of the world and mark my words, it is not!"

"Mother, stop!" C.J. had never heard her father snap at Nana Jean before.

"No way can I afford this. We have to do the right thing and let Chance go," he said, lowering his tone and turning away from

C.J., in a feeble attempt to conceal his words.

But C.J. heard and gasped. There it was; the hateful words had spilled out into the open.

C.J.'s gasp was like a knife cutting through her father's heart. He looked at her, eyes moist. She had never seen him look so defeated or small before.

"Pip, I am so sorry. I wish I was rich. I wish I could make Chance well, but I can't and we have to think about what's best for him."

Then turning to his mother, he spoke harshly for only the second time in 35 years. "Is that enough real life for you Mother?"

The tiny woman walked over to her son and gently put a hand on his anguished face.

"Oh my darling, what you need to know is that you can't afford not to do this. What happens next forever shapes this child we all love."

C.J.'s Dad stood speechless, stuck on the horns of a dilemma.

Nana Jean just smiled and slipped an emerald ring with two stunning shoulder diamonds from her aged finger. C.J.'s father fought off a wave of emotion, and just for a moment you could see the little boy buried deep within the grown man.

"Grandmother's ring. You can't part with that. I can't let you."

"I am an old woman son. What use have I for such baubles? I have lived long enough to know the sparkle in this child's eyes when she looks at that great black pup is worth more than the cold glint of light from this polished stone."

"And besides, your grandmother gave this to me for luck. In many ways it has brought me luck. Now it is time to pass the luck on."

She placed the ring in the palm of her son's hand and closed his fingers around it.

"Take this bauble son and buy us something that is genuinely precious. Buy this great black pup who owns your daughter's heart another chance."

Chapter Nineteen ♣ *A Man Called Roy*

And so the day was saved by a gem as green and sparkling as that Emerald Isle, Ireland, and a wee Irish woman balancing her weight upon an unusual walking stick fashioned after the head of the great hound who claims that far-off land as home.

While Chance remained at the clinic with Dr. P. Peters, the pale yellow house with the green trim at the edge of the great forest was so very hollow and empty.

C.J, her Mom, her Dad and even little Jo-Jo had grown accustomed to the thunk-tha-thunk of Chance's tail upon the floor and his deep "bwoof" "bwoof" whenever a knock came at the door.

Every day C.J.'s Dad drove her to Dr. P. Peter's clinic to be with Chance for if she didn't see him even one day, she felt sure her heart would break.

Dr. P. Peters would scoop the great, black Irish wolfhound up as if he were as light as a feather and carry him out to a blanket in the side yard of the clinic. There under the sheltering canopy of an old maple, the pair would wile away the afternoon; the best of friends through thick or thin.

C.J. stroked the noble head of her very best friend and talked to him of matters only little brown-haired girls and great black dogs are privy to.

Then she would open one of her favourite storybooks and read to Chance. He would rest his great black head in her lap and close his deep brown eyes as the images from the girl's storybook danced across his dreams. Sometimes it was hard to tell where girl ended and dog began, so close was the bond between the two.

As the afternoon's long shadows fell across the lawn of the side yard, Dr. P. Peters would retrieve the pair. Chance would go to his little room in the clinic with his bed and toys and a pyjama top of C.J.'s that he loved to sleep with because it smelled so good, just like her.

C.J. would go back to the yellow house with the green trim at the edge of the great forest, to her family and her room ... her very empty room. After her Mom had tucked her in, read a story and sung the Yellow Bird song, C.J. would reach out from under the bedclothes and pull the blanket Chance slept on into bed with her.

Surrounded by the sweet scent that was Chance, she drifted off to sleep. Chance met her there in her dreams and child and dog would romp until daybreak pulled them feet first back into the real world.

The journey back to health can have many winding ways before one finds the right road home. What is important is that you carry on until you find yourself at long last back at that place your heart knows best.

Chance had his surgery. The news was good; and the news was bad. The left leg was repaired. It was good as new; maybe even better. The right leg was another story. It was worse. So instead of coming home after his big operation, Chance had to stay at the clinic to be cared for by Dr. P. Peters and his staff.

These days Dr. P. Peters, who loved Chance almost as much as the little brown-haired girl did, was kept busy on the telephone calling on the best veterinary medical minds. Each call he made, the question was the same: "What would you do with a leg that will not heal."

After many days and a hundred phone calls, he knew the answer.

One day as C.J. and Chance sat beneath the old maple tree wiling away a soft sunny afternoon, a lanky southern gentleman named Roy stopped by. Dr. P. Peters introduced Roy to C.J. and Chance then went back inside to see his next patient.

It seemed funny to C.J., this stranger dropping by to talk with a girl and her dog. There he was all the same.

"Hi ya all," Roy said with a southern drawl and a smile that made you want to smile right back. He walked over and leaned against the tree trunk. Watching him C.J. thought maybe he moved a little stiffly.

"Would you like to sit down here with us?" she asked.

"Well that's very kind, but if it's all the same to you, I think I'd better stand," Roy said. He had a kind of inner laughter or happiness in his eyes not all people have. C.J. liked that.

Roy bent over and knocked on his right leg with his fist. Odd thing to do, C.J. thought. Odder still was the sound it made.

Roy winked and lifted his pant leg. C.J.'s eyes got wide and her jaw gaped open in disbelief for she was looking at the very first wooden leg she'd ever seen. Even Chance tilted his head in wonder. Roy just smiled at the girl and her great dog and their wide-eyed surprise.

"Have you ever seen anything like that before?" he asked C.J., giving the leg one more rap with his knuckles before lower his pant leg.

"What happened to you?" C.J. asked in a whispered voice. One of the wonders of childhood is being able to be more honest than any grownup would dare.

"Oh, when I was young – not as young as you, but young – I had a motorcycle accident. My leg was crushed and although they tried, the doctors couldn't save it."

"Ohhh," said C.J. "I'm so sorry for you."

"Why?" Roy said with a laugh. "You know little darling everybody has some little thing about them that isn't quite perfect."

"Some people have horrible personalities. A horrible personality," Roy said shaking his head. "Now that's what I call a real problem. Me, I'd rather have a bad leg any day than a personality that was phewww." He held his nose and scrunched up his face.

"I never thought of it that way, but yah, you're right," C.J. giggled.

They fell silent for a moment. C.J. looked at this stranger sizing him up. Suddenly she piped up.

"Chance ... my dog Chance has a bad leg."

"Yah, but I hear he's got a great personality," Roy said with a wink.

C.J. giggled with innocent delight. It is a gift some people lose as the years pass.

"You got that right," she said. Roy looked at this child and her dog for a moment. His voice became more serious.

"I gotta be honest with you little darling before I came here today to meet you, I had heard from Dr. P. Peters that this special dog of yours had a great personality but a bad leg. And that got me thinking. It got me thinking that maybe I could help."

"How?" C.J. asked.

"Well, take a look here." He pulled a photo of a miniature donkey from his shirt pocket. "This little fella had a bad leg just like Chance. The doctors thought they might be at the end of what they could do to help. Then someone gave them my number and look at him today."

In the second photo the tiny donkey wore a cast and a peg leg where his bad leg had been.

"Wow!" C.J. said. "How did you do that?"

"Well his owners were very, very brave. They knew he couldn't go on with the leg Mother Nature gave him. So ... and this is the hard part ... they let the vet amputate the bad leg and they let me make him a new leg, a leg that will never let him down."

C.J. sat quietly with her head bowed looking at the photo of the donkey and his new leg. One hand absently stroked Chance who had long since lost interest in the conversation. He snored gently.

Finally, C.J. raised her head and looked the stranger straight in the eyes. "You could do this for Chance?"

"Yes, little darling I sure could with the help of Dr. P. Peters." He ruffled C.J.'s hair as she handed the photo back to him.

That night C.J.'s Mom and Dad sat C.J. down at the kitchen table for a talk. When they sat at the kitchen table, C.J. knew it was a serious family conference.

"C.J., Dr. P. Peters can not make Chance's right leg well again He feels it may never get better. In fact it is getting worse every day," C.J.'s Mom said.

C.J. looked at her parents' serious faces. She wanted to tell them to take a deep breath. She wished they'd smile like Roy. It all didn't seem so scary when you faced it with a smile.

"Mom and Dad, don't worry. I met a man today who can make Chance a new leg," C.J. said this with pride. Usually at such serious talks as this, she only got to listen.

"But you understand, the doctors will have to take Chance's old leg before giving him a new one," her Dad said with such gravity, that C.J. sat back and looked at him for a second before speaking.

Grown-ups sometimes tried so hard that they missed the obvious. That's what C.J. thought staring up at her parents' serious faces.

"But Mom . . . Dad ... Chance's leg doesn't work anymore. The man said the new leg would work forever. Chance could walk again! He could come home!"

"If this is a vote, I vote 'yes' for a new leg for Chance," she said.

Standing in the shadows of the hallway beyond the kitchen entrance Nana Jean smiled and said to no one but herself "out of the mouths of babes. That's my girl!"

The day of the surgery arrived. Dr. P. Peter's held in his skilled and loving hands the door to a better tomorrow. Chance had the greatness of heart to unlock that door and walk forward into that new day.

Chance learned to walk on his new leg within two days. Within a week, he could rollover and lay on his back on the couch with all four legs in the air. It was his favourite way to lie down.

At bedtime, C.J. would pop Chance's new leg off and rub powder and cream where his surgery had been. She stood the man-made leg in the corner of her bedroom and Chance curled

up on his bed to sleep without it.

In the morning, she'd pop it on again and out he'd go into the yard to play. It was that easy.

Sometimes, when Chance played too hard, he'd come to the back door hopping on three legs. C.J. would pretend to scold him for losing his brand new leg.

Inside she would smile knowing it had probably slipped off

and gone flying through the air as Chance charged headlong after one of the black squirrels who lived in the trees of the great green forest near their home.

And so it was, that Chance came to live happily ever after in the pale yellow house at the edge of the great forest. He was everything Cindy had ever dreamed of when she threw her wish of wishes into the spinning heart of the prancing-pony carousel.

Chance became more than just C.J.'s best friend. He also became a teacher and a good example for children who had lost arms and legs to illness or accident. Dr. P. Peters, C.J. and Chance would visit schools and hospitals to show it could be OK again after something bad happened.

The children's eyes would grow wide when this dog with the peg leg came walking into the room. They would giggle and reach out to touch or hug Chance. And he would let them.

At those moments, they would see this wonderful dog and know in their hearts it really was OK to be different in this world of so many people who tried so hard to be the same.

Chapter 20 ♣ *In a Blink of God's Eye*

Sadly, the season of warm breezes and sunlit fields of play is short indeed for Irish wolfhounds. They say for every one human year, seven years pass in dog time. The clock ticks even faster for the great hound of Ireland.

Some people believe that God so loves the great, gentle Irish wolfhound that he can only bear to let each hound leave his side but briefly.

For only a blink of His eye – seven years of sunrises and sunsets on earth – God lets each hound walk with mortal man. Some he calls home still earlier.

So it is for those mortals who come to love this great hound, winter always comes too soon for their dear friend and the cold heartless wind that blows through the bare branches of trees whispers only one word ... "Good-bye".

As C.J. grew tall and strong, Chance grew old. His black face faded to smoke. He always managed to rally when C.J. returned from school, galloping down the laneway to meet her school bus.

But now instead of chasing squirrels and butterflies, he was happy to curl up beside his very best friend as she sat doing homework or watching TV.

There were moments when he was the pup who'd come in from the storm so many winters ago and she was the girl waiting there for him to be her best friend. But the clock was ticking loud in each of their ears.

Then one day, all too soon, with the sun shining and birds chirping Chance settled down in the front garden of the pale yellow house with the green trim. Small yellow butterflies flitted around. He watched and was happy, but so weary.

He closed his gentle brown eyes and rested in a glorious shaft of sunlight. There in that place where he had loved and been loved deeply, Chance dreamed a happy dream in which he and his brown-haired girl strolled up a hillside painted white and purple with daisies and wild asters.

It was a lovely dream from which he did not wake, for the seven years of sunrises and sunsets had come and gone and God had called Chance home.

Nana Jean crossed over not long after Chance. C.J. often thought of the wee feisty woman flanked by two Irish wolfhounds; dear Nell who she had in Ireland as a young lass, and Chance. It was somehow comforting to think of Chance in such very good company.

Chance was laid to rest beneath the boughs of a pine tree in the yard of the pale yellow house with the green trim that stood at the edge of the great forest.

C.J. placed a wild grapevine wreath upon his grave and planted bleeding hearts and creeping thyme all around. C.J.'s Dad made her a little bench and she sat there many long hours reading and remembering and thinking how lucky she was to have loved and been loved by someone so special.

She wore a silver heart-shaped locket with the word "believe" inscribed on the back and a lock of Chance's hair tucked away inside.

One night not long after Chance left her, C.J. lay in the hollowness of the room they had shared. Sleep would not come. She tossed and turned. Finally, she drifted off to sleep clutching the heart-shaped locket in her hand.

As she crossed over from the waking world to the land of dreams where all things are possible and where prancing-pony carousels spin brightly making wishes come true, C.J. found her Chance again.

Shading her eyes from the sunlight, all C.J. saw at first was a small black dot in a sea of waving field grasses. What was this apparition? She squinted trying to make out what it was that was moving her way so fast. In a breath, her heart saw clearly what her eyes could not.

"|Chance?" she called.

"Bwoof," came the unmistakeable reply. He bwoofed again and opened his mouth in a broad smile. Some people don't think dogs smile, but anyone who truly knows dogs can vouch for the fact they really do.

In another breath, he was there by her side. C.J. dropped to her knees and buried her face in his coat. There was no better scent on heaven or earth than this.

"I love you Chance. You are my heart." He showered her with wet kisses, which she took to mean "me too" in Dog Talk.

They sat together under the draping boughs of willow trees bordering the rippling river that stood between their two worlds. Together they passed the day like this in the absolutely blissful state of doing nothing but sharing each other's company.

Then as the sun set, Chance nudged C.J. and heaved a great sigh. He gave her a look that was wise and knowing. C.J. understood. It was time. Chance had to cross back over the rippling river. She had to return to the world.

"It's Ok boy. You go on ahead. I'll catch up one of these days."

He gave her one last kiss that started at the tip of her chin and ended at her hairline. Then he turned and trotted away through the tall wavy field grass.

"Chance don't ever forget I love you." C.J. called to him. He stopped just this once to turn and look back at her.

"Bwoof! Bwoof!" He answered. C.J. of course, knew this meant "Me too!"

Then he continued through the sea of waving grasses until he was a speck, and then still further until he was no more. For the first time, she realized Chance was moving on four perfect legs, and although tears burned her eyes, her heart smiled.

C.J. woke from her dream to the sunlight of a new day shining through her bedroom window. The dream was so real. She could still feel her face tingle from that last kiss. The heart-shaped locket was still clutched in her hand. Sitting up in bed, she slipped it over her head.

Closing her eyes, she repeated the inscription on the back "believe".

Clutching the locket even tighter, she vowed a vow as passionate and pure as the marvellous wish that had brought

Chance to her.

"Chance you are my heart. And I believe ... I really do believe that I will find my heart again one day." And that is how C.J. found the strength to carry on.

Chance was not the last dog to live in the pale yellow house with green trim at the edge of the great forest. Eventually, another dog came to again fill the home with the pitter-patter of paws. It is a sound every house should have.

Rowdy was a mixed breed; some said part terrier, some said part spaniel. Dad said part trouble and the other part calamity. She was cute and endearing, but she never became C.J.'s special friend. She could never fill the paw prints Chance had left behind. But then those were awful big paw prints to fill.

Still whether we know it or not, in the depth of winter's cruel grasp, the seeds of the future lay in quiet wait for their moment of awakening.

Chance could not stay with C.J. His time on earth was through, but he had left behind with his little brown-haired girl a gift and a key to the future.

The things C.J. learned from Dr. P. Peters about caring for Chance had turned her mind into a sponge eager to absorb the knowledge she would need to one day help others the way Dr. P. Peters had helped Chance.

She wanted to grow-up to be everything Dr. P. Peters was because like her Nana Jean, he knew what wonders were possible if only you dared to believe against all reason and against all odds.

So one day she went to university far, far way from the pale yellow house with the green trim at the edge of the great forest to study veterinary medicine.

She could do this because a tiny, Irish woman told her that if she believed, all things were possible, and because she carried in her heart the love of an Irish wolfhound called Chance.

Chapter 21 ♣ *Worlds Merge*

So it was that C.J. grew from a child into a woman. Through all those years and all those miles, she carried the memory of Chance in her heart as clear and true as the first day their lives had joined.

And though this was good, she longed for the touch of him, the smell of him and the sweet sight of him, but despite her deepest desire, he was nowhere to be found.

Still, there are times when the iron wall between the mortal world and the one beyond turn to gossamer.

On those days, when the elements of the earth brew together in just the right way, January winds can blow May warm and Mother Nature can drop her grim winter gaze to briefly grace the world with the beauty of her smile.

In the fertile cusp of such moments, there is magic to be found. Though she didn't know it, for C.J. just such a moment was at hand.

For those who have loved pure and deep ... for those whose love still burns despite time and barriers, there can come creeping without notice a moment when stout spirits again find one another.

It is the power of pure hearts to transcend the plane they are assigned to and to send proof of life. So for a moment or an hour or a day, one whispers like the wind through the other.

Not quite an embrace, it is more like the promise of an

embrace. Like someone brushing past you. You feel their presence for a breath and then they are gone.

In one sense, it leaves you wanting. It rips cruelly at the heart opening old wounds of loss. But it also bridges the gap of time and space and makes fresh all that was fading. It fuels the embers of love that still burn and it gives the promise there will be another time ... another place

C.J. woke from a dream of Chance. She woke with a smile but her pillow was wet with tears. She looked at the photo of the beautiful black Irish wolfhound on her nightstand.

She wondered would she ever wake without expecting to reach down and stroke the noble brow of the one, who for so long, had kept guard at her bedside as she slept. She hoped not.

C.J. swung her feet out of bed and stretched her arms to the sky. The alarm clock beside the framed photo of Chance said 6 a.m. Another day; a busy day. Tuesday mornings she had a full slate of surgeries followed by afternoon appointments.

She had jumped though all the hoops, learned all the anatomy ... all the diseases and their cures. She had mastered the formulas and after all of that had discovered the toughest part of a vet's job was not the science but the people. The animals she understood.

The people were sometimes a mystery; sometimes a disappointment. Then there were those who cared for their animals as she had cared for Chance. These people and the long and growing list of animals helped made it all OK.

The bedroom door burst open and a whirlwind of giggles and long, brown curls swept across the room and into her arms.

"Mommy! Mommy! Daddy made waffles for breakfast. Come on!"

The little brown-haired girl now had her own brown-haired angel. Time had flown and so had so many of those she loved

Not long after C.J. finished her studies, C.J.'s mom fell ill and struggled two years to hang on to life before surrendering her spirit to the fact that it was time to journey on. In his grief and emptiness, C.J.'s Dad fell ill and followed two years later.

He passed without fighting the fact. Even in his final days of pain and physical indignity, he found the joy in spirit to laugh.

He slid away from this world with an easy grace so as not to make too much trouble for those around him.

It was the final lesson he had to offer his little brown-haired girl. It was perhaps the most important lesson of all.

C.J.'s sister, little Jo-Jo, lived in a big city far away. Though they were sisters, their worlds did not often merge these days as is often the way of the adult world.

But life has a design that we are privy to only on a need-to-know basis which means until things are about to unfold, the scheme of it all is not laid at our feet and perhaps that is best.

The arrival of Richard was certainly a surprise. He showed up at her clinic one day with a dog he found injured at the side of the road. .

The dog had tags on its collar, so the owner could be traced, but had this passing stranger not cared enough to stop, it could have died from shock. Richard had wrapped the injured dog in his expensive down-lined parka.

He paid for the emergency surgery to repair a fractured femur while clinic staff worked to track down the dog's people. He did it without knowing if the owners would be found and if found whether they would reimburse him. He did it because he cared.

C.J. looked at this man with the dark hair and dark eyes and thought she caught a whisper of tall pine trees and quiet back roads. Something about him felt like home.

He looked at her and thought he sensed the forest at nightfall and a path strewn with pine needles, traveled more by the swift-footed fox and curious raccoon than by man. He looked at this woman and wondered why the deep forest behind the green of her eyes felt like home.

The injured dog survived. His owners were found. It turned out his name was Ralphie. To C.J. he would always be Cupid; and with good reason. C.J. and Richard married the very next spring.

New people now lived in the pale yellow house with green trim at the edge of the great forest, but they were kind. So the little-brown haired girl went home to her roots to say her vows of love for the man called Richard.

That day, as the spring breeze stirred the pine branches and rustled the leaves of the poplars, Cindy felt Chance and Nana Jean close by. And she knew her Mom and Dad were standing right there with them.

They say you can never go home again, but really you never leave home behind. It is something you carry with you in every fibre of your being.

Chapter Twenty-two ♣ *The Circle is Complete*

As is so often the way of the world, Richard and C.J. in time felt the urge to fill their little nest of a home with one other. They had a daughter who they named Rae-Ann. Along with many sleepless nights, she brought them joy and laughter and a sense of renewal.

Rae-Ann grew up hearing stories of the great black Irish wolfhound Chance. She knew the black dog in the photo on Mommy's nightstand was Chance. And she knew, in the way little children who have not yet been programmed by the greater world know, that somewhere in her Mommy's heart Chancey lived on.

Funny, she thought, that Mommy and Daddy hadn't gotten her a dog. Rae-Ann hoped with the pure heart of a child who believes all things possible, that someday a puppy would come to be with her, and to mean as much as Chance did to her Mommy.

And just as C.J. had learned from her Irish nana ... Rae-Ann had learned from her Mommy that if you truly believe without any shadow of doubt, dreams can come true.

It was a blustery day as C.J. drove to the clinic. She thought, of another January when high winds blew and the scratch of a paw on the front door of the pale yellow house with the green trim at the edge of the great forest had changed her life forever.

In a season that seemed to be a heartless stretch of cold, ice and snow, there could occasionally come the most awesome surprises. As she tucked her chin into the collar of her coat walking from the car park to the back door of the clinic, she tried to remember this.

Inside, she shucked off her coat and boots and slipped on her white jacket with her name tag. D.V.M. the letters followed her name, Doctor of Veterinary Medicine. Sometimes she couldn't believe she had made it.

She loved the clinic in the quiet times before the rush of clients coming and going. It was then – early morning or late in the day – that you could feel it had a heartbeat of its own. If you stood very still with your eyes closed, you could pick up the pulse and as all good doctors know, where there's a pulse, there's hope.

The animals booked for today's surgery were all checked in. Staff had started to prep the first. It was routine today, two spays, three neuters, lunch and then office calls.

Several hours later, with the ebb and flow of another day behind her, C.J. stood again in the back area of the clinic. The last staff member had slipped through the front door ten minutes before.

C.J. turned the lock behind her. A couple of the surgeries were staying overnight. They were still woozy and dozed away in their individual cages dreaming of their own homes and their own people. Someone would be back to check on them later.

C.J. looked at them, understanding. "It's OK little ones. Tomorrow you'll be home and this scary memory will fade."

With a sigh, she slipped her coat and boots on, dimmed the lights and stepped out into the darkness. Only six p.m. and dark. That was the other thing C.J. missed at this time of year - sunlight.

The wind whipped around C.J.'s head as she fiddled with the lock on the back door. She cursed, frozen metal bolts that did not want to drop into place without grumbling at the cold.

Head bowed to keep the sideways blast of driving snow from stinging her eyes, C.J. made her way across the car park to find her midnight blue SUV buried.

"January ..." she muttered under her breath as though it was the most vile utterance possible.

She pushed the instant entry control, and turned the engine on to warm the vehicle. Rummaging inside, she found the snowbrush. It was buried under a stack of newspapers she'd meant to drop off at the recycling depot two days earlier.

"There you are," she said.

Six inches of fluffy snow covered the SUV. 'Ok, first the roof', C.J. thought making giant swipes. The snow scattered or caught in the wind and carried off. Some caught in a cross wind and blew back into her face. It was cold and fresh.

Tired, cold and intent on the task at hand, C.J. almost didn't notice the bump in the snow at the edge of the SUV's front bumper. Of course, in these weather conditions, with the world whipped into a white wilderness, it was hard to recognize anything.

Just before falling over the bump, C.J. stopped and stared right down at it. She would never be able to explain what she felt at that moment. It was like a mind chill when you eat ice cream too fast, or when something happens that freezes you in time.

Her mind was saying to her: "This bump is wrong. This bump should not be here."

All her senses were telling her, there was something terribly out of place about this bump here at her feet. C.J. crouched down, and gently ran the snowbrush over top of the bump.

"Oh my gosh!" she gasped. The strip of missing snow revealed black hair ... lovely, wavy black hair.

She threw the brush aside, tore off her gloves and with bare hands brushed the rest of the snow away. There curled up in a fetal position was a very, large black pup. It had taken shelter from the wind under the edge of her SUV's bumper. Its pulse was weak; its respiration shallow.

"Hey, hey little one. What are you doing out alone on a night like this?" Her words caught in her throat recalling another black pup and another frozen winter's eve so long ago.

C.J. was strong, but the pup was huge. She couldn't lift him alone. Turning off the car, she raced through the biting wind and stinging ice pellets. She thought that an old comforter used to line crates for her larger patients might work.

Back outside, she rolled the pup onto the doubled-over comforter. He groaned. She felt relief at hearing him respond. The distance between her parking spot and the clinic backdoor had never seemed farther away than it did right now.

She tugged on the two sides of the comforter and gently dragged the still pup across the parking area. A couple times, the comforter started to slip out from under him and she had to stop and kneel down in the snow to shift him back to the centre.

She had to stop breathless from exertion, and the strange way her heart was pounding in her head was like someone knocking on a door asking to come in.

Finally they made it, this dark-haired woman who loved animals and this giant black pup who had come to the edge of the abyss and almost given up on the world before his time.

Inside C.J. slammed the metal door shut with a thud. The wind howled outside but inside the calming hum of the clinic – that soothing pulse - took over.

C.J. grabbed extra blankets and the heat lamp. She rubbed the pup's paws. No frostbite. He lay still, not opening his eyes.

"Come on boy. Come on back to me." She ran her healing hands over him, and was flooded with a sense of deja vu. She could not miss noticing how good it felt to run her hands through the dark coarse hair still soaked from being buried in the snow.

The pup shuddered. It was a shudder that rippled through him from his head to his toes to the tip of his tail. Then he sighed and groaned. It was like watching a hibernating bear stir from the depth of a winter's slumber.

C.J. had called the pup back. Good dog that he was, he had obeyed.

The pink tongue slipped out to lick her hand and the tail went 'thunk-a-thunk-a-thunk'. It was a sound C.J. hadn't heard for quite sometime despite her many dog clients.

There was only one dog she'd ever met whose tail could beat out that happy sound. Dark eyes opened just a slit to check out the world.

C.J. sat back on her heels for a moment in absolute dismay. She had been so caught up in the moment; she hadn't let the fact filter from the back of her mind into her conscious being.

But this was no ordinary pup. This was the great dog of Ireland. This was an Irish wolfhound pup as black and beautiful as the one she had loved so long ago and every day since his passing.

Not since that night when as a little brown-haired girl C.J. had dared to creep down the hall from her bedroom to stand on a stool peering over her parents' shoulder, had she seen anything so utterly, breathtakingly, perfect and amazing.

C.J. leaned back in toward the pup, who had held her in his gaze from the moment he opened his eyes. He wriggled in a bit closer too and dropped his noble giant head into her lap. She gasped out loud ... it was an expression of joy torn from the deepest chambers of the heart where we covet those things most sacred.

As she leaned in closer, the pup licked her face from the chin to the top of her forehead. She buried her face in the wavy black hair on his neck and breathed deep the sweet musky scent of Irish wolfhound, a scent she had missed these many, many years.

An hour later, she pulled into the driveway of the little farmhouse where she, Richard and Rae-Ann lived. The pup sat on the bench seat behind her with two comforters draped over him.

"Ok little man, get ready to meet the family," C.J. said, looking in the rear view mirror at the picture of contentment.

If she had stayed an hour later working at the clinic, she wasn't so sure those deep dark eyes would be looking at her right now. But they were ... they were ... and something inside of her that had been still and quiet was suddenly awake.

She knew he probably was lost. Someone was probably looking for him. But then, they thought that about Chance, and he had come to stay and love and be loved for as many seasons as he could.

She was afraid to hope ... and yet she hoped. It was her way, and somewhere on the other side of the river that divides the worlds, a little Irish woman smiled with pride at the knowledge.

The farmhouse was warm. It wasn't perfectly clean or perfectly decorated. Yet it was simply perfect. It resonated with the love and trust that now lived inside its 150-year-old walls.

Down the hallway, bubbled the happy sounds of Richard and Rae-Ann preparing dinner, discussing the process, every step of the way. The great, black pup sat by C.J.'s side as she shed her boots, scarf and coat.

C.J. crouched down beside the pup and whispered in his ear, "Ok, little man, it's show time." She stood up and called out, "Hello, I'm home. Where are my kisses? Where are my hugs?"

Hitting an octave only ever achieved by five-year-old girls or opera sopranos, Rae-Ann squealed, "Mommy! It's Mommy!"

"Steady boy," C.J. said, resting a hand on the black pup's shoulder. "You're about to experience the whirlwind known as Rae-Ann."

Squeals, curls and giggles rounded the kitchen corner and headed down the hall. Richard came behind. The gentle smile that shone through his eyes as much as on his lips chased away the January chill.

About halfway down the hall, father and daughter were stopped in their tracks by the sight of a giant black pup sitting politely at C.J.'s side with his tail going 'thunk-a-thunk-a-thunk' against the hardwood floor.

"Guys, I have someone I'd like you to meet" C.J. said crouching beside the pup.

Rae-Ann came close. Close enough that she and the pup were nose to nose. It was too great a target for the pup to resist. Out came the tongue and Rae-Ann had the first Irish wolfhound face washing of her young life.

She shrieked in surprise and utter glee, and who would not!

The pup knew he had done well and the tail started up again, this time sideways going 'thunk-a-thunk-thunk' against C.J.'s leg and the hall wall.

Rae-Ann threw her arms around the pup's neck and said "Chance! It's Chancey!"

"Oh ... Rae-Ann, honey. Chancey had to go away a long time ago. This puppy is like him ... very like him, but it's not him."

The pup looked up at C.J. with a strange expression she couldn't quite read. Rae-Ann was not bothered by her Mother's words. She had lived long enough to know there were things grownups could not possibly understand.

"Come on Chancey," she called and the pup followed her down the hall chasing after the tea towel she trailed across the floor behind her.

C.J. watched the beautiful sight of her darling dark-haired daughter and the giant black pup together as though they were part of the same puzzle that only now could be complete. She knew the feeling all too well.

Her fingers automatically rose to her throat and sought out the necklace she wore with the strands of Chance's hair and the single word "Believe".

But she had been an adult for such a long time now and the world has a way of shaping even those whose hearts beat pure. Richard's eyes met hers.

"I'll tell you guys all about it over dinner. It's the strangest thing…" C.J. said.

Down the hall in the brightly-lit kitchen, Rae-Ann squealed in delight and the pup answered "Bwoof ... bwoof."

"Oh, oh. I think that bears investigating." Richard said.

The moment felt so right. Somewhere inside C.J. the child who believed was knocking on the door of the grownup who had had to learn the ways of the world in order to survive.

"You bet!" C.J. said, and the two adults headed down the hall to see if it was merriment or mischief child and dog were up to.

That night after Rae-Ann was tucked away in bed, the great black pup curled up on the couch by C.J. Richard sat in a deep armchair across the room and thought his wife had never looked happier.

As wolfhounds are so inclined to do, the pup soon gave a stretch and a sigh and rolled over on his back to snooze contentedly with all four, very long legs in the air. It was only then that C.J. noticed the pup's chest.

Most Irish wolfhounds have a white blaze on their chest. This pup had something quite special indeed. "Richard, look! Look at his chest!"

The pup's blaze formed a perfect heart and that heart framed a second heart. The second heart was black not white. Two perfect hearts; different but joined like she and Chance.

The facts are in. The world is not flat. We do not fall off the edge and disappear if we travel too far. It is a continuous circle and if you travel long enough, you will again visit that place where you set out from.

Looking at the two hearts blazing forth from this pup's chest, C.J.'s own words bounced around inside her head defying logic and demanding to be heard.

"Chance, you are my heart," she whispered and the pup rolled back on his side and settled his gaze on her.

"I must be crazy," she said, shaking her head. The pup did not break his gaze. He was ready to wait out her resistance.

C.J. reached out to gently stroke his lovely head and whispered, this time so only he could hear, "You are my heart!"

A pink tongue licked the hand that stroked and lovely black lips curled back in a toothy grin. Suddenly C.J. knew. She simply knew, for the second time in her life, that the words her Irish nana had spoken were true.

"Two hearts so true can not be torn asunder as long as you believe, child. With all your heart ... with all the fire in you ... believe."

In the softness of the glow from the fire, with her darling daughter down the hall, the man she loved across the room and the dog who owned her heart at her side, C.J. said the words out loud .

"I believe."

And somewhere far and away, beyond the weeping willow and the river that divides the worlds, a wee Irish woman patted the head of a great black Irish wolfhound named Nell, and smiled.

"Aye, my darling Nell," she said with a visage that was young again. "So it is ... So it is. The circle comes full way 'round and two pure hearts rejoin."

"Here we stand together again you and I... And the dance has come full circle for C.J. and her darling Chance. As I knew, in my heart of hearts, it would."

"But you know darling Nell 'tis not my doing alone. 'Tis the way of the Irish. Somewhere on the sod of dear old Ireland, it is carved in stone that forevermore the guiding compass of two hearts that beat true will steer a safe course home."

Throwing her arms around the wolfhound's great breadth of neck she sighed a sigh of contentment.

"Home. Ah, this is my home, Nell. Wherever thee be. I would chase your tail through a thousand lifetimes just to catch stride of you and again be by your side."

Although the translation between people-talk and wolfhound-talk remains an inexact science, it is believed that when Nell "bwoofed" back a bwoof so deep and resonate it almost carried across the river, past the weeping willow and back to where C.J. and Chance slumbered by the fire, her meaning was simple and clear.

It went something like this ... "Ah Jean, you too are my heart, my home, my happiness."

Then again wolfhounds, though great of heart, can be slight of word. So without the embellishment of human interpretation what Nell said may in fact only have been "Me too! Me too!"

Either way, in the end it's all the same. Shamrocks... and rainbows ... and shattered dreams all mended new. For love pure and true is the one pot of gold that can make the broken whole again. Believe it!

And if anyone asks where you heard such a tale, tell them you have it on good authority.

An Irish wolfhound told you so. ♣♣

Do not stand by my grave and weep;

I am not there. I do not sleep.

I am a thousand winds that blow.

I am the diamond glints on snow.

I am the sunlight on ripened grain.

I am the gentle autumn's rain.

When you awaken in the morning's hush,

I am the swift uplifting rush of quiet birds in circled flight.

I am the soft stars that shine at night.

Do not stand at my grave and cry;

I am not there. I did not die.

*Ojibwa Prayer.

To learn more about Irish Wolfhounds,

contact any of the following:

The Irish Wolfhound Club of Canada

The Irish Wolfhound Club of America Inc.

The Irish Wolfhound Club of Great Britain

The Irish Wolfhound Club of Ireland

Each has a web site that can be reached by querying
their name.

Cindy Krieg (Nuttall) was born in Temagami, Ontario, in a house her father and grand-father built. The author's roots are firmly in Northern Ontario. Her family moved to North Bay, Ont., when she was young. Growing up in rural Northern Ontario, the author's first friends were the animals in the forest surrounding her family home and stray dogs who would appear from time to time at the end of the laneway leading to their door. This early connection bred a long-life interest in the possibility for better communication and better understanding between species, specifically mankind and the fellow creatures with which people are intended to share the world.

Her first full-time stint as a daily paper reporter was with The North Bay Nugget. She later worked for both The Peterborough Examiner and The Ontario Farmer and two of its agriculture–based trade magazines.

The author now lives on a 72-acre farm called 'Grayspirit', just south of Peterborough, Ont. She lives with three Irish wolfhounds, two Scottish deerhounds, a bevy of cats, and the residents of a converted drive shed which these days is a horse barn. The barn residents of Grayspirit Farm include a miniature stallion called Willy, two Icelandic geldings, Numi and Funi, two aged mares, Secret, an America Saddlebed, and Lacey, a Morgan. Then there is Pip aka Gypsy Rose and Barbie, two miniature mares.

Her next project is about the Wild Cats of Stewart Hall, a colony of feral cats who were born, lived and died in the tall grass and winding paths at Grayspirit long before the author arrived.

Also in the works is a story about an Icelandic horse called Funi, a misunderstood soul who finds the love of a girl can lead him down the path he must travel in order to overcome his paralyzing fear and mistrust of man.

Janet Griffin-Scott was born in Toronto but was raised in Midland, Ontario, where she had an outlet for her love of horses and nature at an early age. As a teenager, Janet owned, trained and showed horses. She attended York University's BFA program and majored in Graphic Design, Photography and Illustration. She then worked in downtown Toronto in Ad agencies and art studios as a freelance artist for the next ten years. During that time she married her husband James, who she had met in high school when he tutored her in math, her only bad subject.

When Janet and her husband James' children started school Janet decided to pursue her first love of subject matter in art, horses. In high school and then in university, she had been discouraged to paint anything to do with horses. Her art teacher in Grade Nine art gave her a near failing grade when he was so frustrated at her turning every assignment into an equine art project. Finally free to pursue her desire to portray horses, Janet experimented with different media: pencil, oil, acrylic and finally a mixture of watercolour and gouache. She found that she could get incredible effects with the mixed media, achieving effects that were soft and subtle to bold and brilliant. Janet began a ten year journey to perfect and hone her craft, doing commissioned portrait of dogs, cats, children and horses. During this time she sold originals and prints in several horsey venues such as The Royal Winter Fair in Toronto and Spruce Meadows in Calgary.

Janet then began to put more of her work into print, as prints, Greeting Cards and gradually an ever increasing line of equine giftware. Janet has joined the lucrative world of Licensing, whereby companies license her work for their own products.

Janet rides and trains horses regularly, and competes in 25 mile Competitive Trail Rides. In 1999 Janet and her family realized a dream to move to the country and purchased ten acres of land where they built a small hobby farm. "Horses are such noble creatures" says Janet. "They combine athleticism and beauty, grace and power in an unbelievably powerful way. Their highly developed social behaviour and friendly social natures make them great companions. There is nothing more wonderful than tuning into their communication and being accepted as one of the herd. From their warm brown eyes and fuzzy winter coats to their shiny summer beauty, they have become essential to my life and happiness. I hope to portray a small touch of this great respect and love for horses in my artwork."

No Character in this novel is patterned after any one individual.

Each is a mosaic of attributes borrowed from people who have passed through my life, spiced with imagination and polished with the shammy cloth of creative licence.

... That is except for Grayspirit's Come by Chance.

There was indeed an Irish Wolfhound named Chance who we at Grayspirit Farm were privileged to have known and loved.

Chance left an indelible pawprint on our lives. He taught me what it is to be great of heart. So it is from the magic of our moments together, I have caste the web of memory and inspiration and spun forth the tale of an Irish dog called Chance

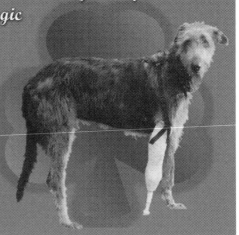

Grayspirit's
Come By
Chance

"The Champ"
1997-2002

♣♣Special Thanks♣♣

Just as it takes a village to raise a child, it also takes many seeds of inspiration to transport a literary work into being.

First I must thank Grayspirit's Come By Chance "The Champ" who took me along on his five-year, tumultuous journey through this mortal plane, and in doing so, taught me much about life, love , bravery, and letting go.

I must thank my husband Philip for introducing me to the amazing breed known as the Irish wolfhound, and for building a life together that always included our hounds. I also thank my daughter Kelly and grand-daughter Lexy for providing the inspiration for the main human character in the book.

I thank my friend Cathy Grixti for pointing the way when Chance was in need and for finding us the real-life Roy (Scudamore), of Equine Prosthetics, who helped put our little man back together again.

Finally I offer undying thanks and gratitude to two special people without whom Chance would not have had ... a chance.

Dr. Peter Gould D.V.M., of Brealey Drive Animal Clinic, and his partner in practice and life Gillian Baker. These two special people spread wings of care and love over our family in a dark time lighting the way with hope and friendship above and beyond. There are no words ... . C.J.